I Am Not a Wolf

With special thanks to

Jad Abi-Mansour, Luke Gill, Chris Gozali, Zach Hulesch,

Alex Kazer, Eddie Song and Brandon Woodle

I Am Not a Wolf

Dan Sheehan and Sage Coffey

unbound

First published in 2020

Unbound

6th Floor Mutual House, 70 Conduit Street, London W1S 2GF

www.unbound.com

Text Design by Ellipsis, Glasgow

A CIP record for this book is available from the British Library

ISBN 978-1-78352-932-2 (limited edition)
ISBN 978-1-78352-933-9 (trade pbk)
ISBN 978-1-78352-934-6 (ebook)

Printed in Great Britain by Clays Ltd, Elcograph S.p.A
1 3 5 7 9 8 6 4 2

To Mom, Dad, and Becca
for their encouragement, support, and unending
tolerance for my use of the phrase 'wolf twitter'

YOU'RE SCARED. You knew today was coming, but you thought it would be easier to do what needs to be done. You thought you'd find yourself overwhelmed with adrenaline and ready to complete the task at hand. You know nothing happens without hard work. Your mother used to say that the only guarantee any living thing has is that each moment of its life will be spent in a desperate fight to justify its existence. If she saw you now, she'd tell you that you're a coward. She'd tell you that if you were going to do this, you'd have already done it. She'd wonder why you were even bothering. But your mother isn't here, and today you're going to do it. Today, you're going to take a shower.

You are a wolf. But this is something the world can't know. Some people aren't ready to know, some aren't willing to understand, but most are just terrified of wolves for some reason. You've spent much of your life integrating into human society. You have a job, an apartment, several online dating profiles, and a terrible roommate. But human beings are expected to maintain a certain level of cleanliness that you've let fall by the wayside. You refuse to risk sacrificing all that hard work just because you fear running water.

It's time to make this right. You ease your paws over the shower knob and gently move it to the left. The shower sputters to life, spraying harmless water into the tub. You watch the water run into the drain and glance back at the showerhead. Harmless. You leap into the tub and the water strikes you. At first you bristle at the sudden warmth, but you take a deep breath and allow yourself to relax. It's just water. You're safe and soon, you'll be clean too. You don't find yourself showering often and you're certain that your roommate won't miss a little bit of his shampoo, so you wrap your jaws around his bottle of 2-in-1 shampoo and conditioner. All you need to do is get a little bit of it on the floor of the tub so that you can evenly distribute it across your fur and bestow upon yourself the smell of 'fresh rain' or at least its chemical approximation. You ease your jaw shut to squeeze the shampoo when suddenly, the water gets hot. It shoots from a comfortable lukewarm temperature to something more along the line of hot knives and you suddenly feel extremely uncomfortable. Caleb must have started the dish-washer in the kitchen. Your jaw clamps down instinctively on the shampoo bottle with incredible pressure, causing your mouth to fill with a goop that tastes nothing like rain as the shampoo explodes into your eyes. You howl in rage and sprint out of the tub, blind. You run through what must be the shower curtain and tumble out of the bathroom and into the living room. Still completely wrapped in the shower curtain, you run toward what smells like your room and violently shut the door behind you. You escape the shower curtain and shake yourself dry, taking a moment to note that while you've definitely ruined the bathroom in a big way, you do smell less like dirt now. You really hope your roommate didn't see that.

Speaking of which, it's time for breakfast and, based on the nightmarish smell you've just caught on the air, Caleb is making his ridiculous vegan sausage patties again, so you'll be fending for yourself. As if that's a new concept.

YOU POP UP on two legs and begin the complicated process of getting ready for work. Once you've fully dressed yourself, you fiddle with the door until it swings open. You stumble into your living room, briefly dropping down onto all fours and forcing yourself back up again. Your eyes dart around the room to see if you've saved face. It would appear that you have. Caleb is too busy frying up impostor sausage and playing some sort of game on his phone. Caleb is a frail-looking young man. He is tall which often signifies strength in humans, but his form is thin and to you seems malnourished. You assume this is likely the result of countless years of indoorsmanship. He's a young man but seems to not have any sort of job. He often talks about a screenplay that he is 'working on' or 'workshopping' or 'getting some notes on from his friend who works on *Rick & Morty*' but his day-to-day efforts seem mostly dedicated to binge-watching Netflix shows. You are unsure where his money comes from, but he occasionally mentions a temp agency. Caleb's lifestyle and various non-traditional food smells are often annoying, but Caleb has a quality that you value above all others: he has never asked you a single question about your personal life. You walk over to the fridge and wrap your jaws around a rotisserie chicken sitting on the top shelf.

You've managed to integrate into this world because human society is too self-absorbed to pay you much mind. Without any natural predators, the human race has become content to keep most interactions quick and easy. In fact, you've found that the more someone stands out, the more people tend to leave them alone. You recently saw a man dancing shirtless in the street in broad daylight. Not a single person even looked at him, let alone said his behavior was incongruous with that of a normal human. It seems that everyone is terrified that the person who seems 'dance in the street'-interesting might also be 'secret murderer'-interesting. For a moment you think that this is sad before you remember that it also helps you ride the bus.

You gnaw on your morning bird and its bones crack loudly. Caleb's face grimaces but he doesn't avert his gaze from his phone. He doesn't seem to care what type of interesting you are as long as you pay your rent. You worry sometimes that your relationship with Caleb could be better. You do not have many human friends and it would be nice to spend mornings and evenings in something other than odd silence. You think today may be the perfect day to forge your first true human friendship. You are under the impression that true roommates communicate mostly through low-stakes arguments. You clear your throat and prepare to address one of Caleb's many transgressions.

'HELLO CALEB, GOOD MORNING. I WAS WONDERING WHAT YOUR REASON WAS FOR LEAVING THAT BOWL OF

RIGATONI ALFREDO IN THE SINK ALL WEEK WAS BECAUSE
THE CHEESE HAS BEGUN TO SCAB IN A WAY THAT I HAVE
PREVIOUSLY ONLY OBSERVED IN WOUNDS.'

Caleb briefly looks up from his phone. You put on your best
smile, which, if you're being honest with yourself, is mostly just you
leaving your mouth open and panting a little bit.

'Oh yeah. Sorry. I forgot about it. I'll totally get it this afternoon;
I just have a thing to get to this morning.'

Nailed it. Today is going to be amazing. Caleb walks away in a
manner that you assume is more friendly than before. Caleb is a
big-time introvert, he talks about it all the time, so you know that
your friendship may be slower to develop. And he *does* always have
a thing to get to. But today was a big step for the two of you.
Perhaps after work you can address the fact that Caleb has not
purchased any toilet paper for multiple weeks. Interpersonal relationships are a whirlwind! You grab your backpack and head out
the door, determined to conquer the day. Human life is about being
as stressed out as you can possibly get without throwing up, and
today you intend to get extremely close to throwing up.

You walk outside into the cool morning. You can already tell
from the breeze and the scent of grass clippings in the air that it's
going to be a beautiful spring day. You've survived another winter
and it's time to be your best self. You ate your breakfast quickly and
decisively, leaving you with ample time to get to the office. You
could go to work the usual way, by taking the bus, but you consider
the idea of saving yourself some headache by using a rideshare app
to save time.

―――――

If you wish to take the bus, turn to page 9.

If you would like to use a rideshare app, turn to page 19.

YOU MAKE YOUR WAY toward your local bus stop. It's not the fastest way of getting around, but it's certainly the safest. The bus is a horrid place, so full of strangers and various smells that the people riding it make a special effort to pay as little attention to those around them as they possibly can. The bus is a place where everyone stares at the floor and minds their own business and when riding it, you've never felt safer. Your bus stop is fairly empty this morning, with one solitary man waiting on the bench. You walk past him to stand closer to the curb, leaving a healthy distance between the two of you. Bus Stop Code dictates that you both should pretend that the other person is not there for as long as you possibly can.

'Some lovely weather we've been getting, right?'

Sweet Mother Nature, this stranger has broken Bus Stop Code. This man has revealed himself as a loose cannon, as unpredictable as he is dangerous. Now, you must act like talking to a complete stranger isn't completely insane or you risk further questions.

'WOW YES YOU ARE CORRECT I ENJOY HOW NIGHT IS SHORTER DURING THIS TIME OF YEAR BECAUSE THERE IS LESS DARKNESS TO FEAR.'

The man turns to face you, giving you a good look up and down. 'Yeah, wow, I guess that's true. Never really thought about it that way.' Oh no, this is awful; you've accidentally said something he finds thought-provoking. He'll certainly have more to say now. He pauses for a moment, 'In the winter, it's dark, like, a lot.' That was an extremely obvious point he just made, so luckily it doesn't really merit a response. If you play it cool here, you can come off as both intellectually superior and unwilling to continue speaking. You nod your head lightly, to show that you heard that dumb thing he said. If you're lucky, the conversation will end here. You are not lucky.

'It makes me think of when . . . '

Before this interpersonal train wreck can get any worse, the bus pulls up. When the door slides open, you sling your backpack over your shoulder and quickly make your way onto the bus. You take part in the bus ritual of apologizing to literally everyone you pass, and do your best to blend in near the back. You have to put as much distance between yourself and the stranger as you possibly can. You cautiously look around and see no sign of him in the dense crowd of commuters. The bus starts moving, and you let yourself relax just a little bit, when suddenly you hear, 'There he is!' The stranger smiles at you. 'Thought I lost you, bus buddy! So, where're you headed?'

Bus buddy. You now know for a fact that you are on a runaway train straight to hell. The stranger is now right in your personal space, kissing-distance away from your face due to the fullness of the bus, and you have nowhere to go. At this distance, he is sure to notice your many serrated teeth or at the very least your thick coat of facial fur. You are doing your best to remain calm, but you need to make a decision quickly. If you attempt to continue talking to him, you run the risk of him realizing that you're not the man you claim to be. You could attempt to get off at the next stop but then you risk the greatest humiliation of all: being slightly late for work.

———

If you think it's best to indulge the friendly stranger and get to work, turn to page 12.

If you want to be cautious and get off at the next stop, making yourself late, turn to page 15.

EVEN THINKING of the disappointment crossing your boss's face if you came into work late makes you upset. You are a part of the company. You have synergy with those people. You can't just throw that away because you're worried about some bus stranger. Being a human is about asking yourself what's important and understanding that the correct answer to that question is business and business-related activities. You have a job to do and you know that if the roles were reversed, your faceless corporation would NEVER do anything so callous to you. You will talk to this upsetting stranger. For capitalism.

'OH SORRY FRIEND I DID NOT MEAN TO PAUSE SO CONSPICUOUSLY BEFORE ANSWERING YOUR QUESTION, I AM GOING TO MY JOB AS A GRAPHIC DESIGNER AT A BIG-TIME COMPANY.'

'Oh, very cool, where do you work?'

The man is a monster. This is one of the most stressful moments you've ever experienced. You feel hot and anxious. Your heart is buzzing. If your body was a human body, it would be completely covered in sweat right now. But wolves don't sweat, they regulate their body temperature through the far more archaic practice of hanging their tongues out of their mouths and panting, which you have now begun to do. The bus stranger takes a quick look at you and then quickly darts his eyes toward the floor.

'Oh . . . hey, is there any chance you could . . . could you . . . not . . . Uh, I didn't mean to give you the wrong idea but . . . '

Your panting has upset the bus stranger! Of course! This is it; you have a chance to end this polite renegade once and for all!

'HAHA SORRY PAL I AM JUST A CLASSIC BUS PERVERT AND THAT IS A PART OF PUBLIC TRANSIT THAT EVERY-ONE HAS TO DEAL WITH FOR SOME REASON.'

The bus stranger, slowly begins to create more distance between the two of you, and before long, he's completely moved to the other side of the bus, only looking at you occasionally when he thinks you can't see him, as if he only wants to make sure that you aren't attempting to come any closer to him. You've found yourself saved by the staggeringly high rate of public transit sexual harassment! You stand quietly and politely until your stop arrives, making your way off the bus without shooting the stranger so much as a pervert's fare-well glance.

———

Turn to page 24.

AS MUCH AS IT pains you to even consider it, being late for work may be the safest option for you. There's not a soul out there that would doubt your dedication to your entry-level graphic design job. You'd never want to disappoint the company, but if your true identity is outed on this bus, you may never see your desk again. The bus stranger's question hangs in the air. He gives you a confused look. 'I said, where're you headed?'

You need to act now. You hold tight to your backpack and push past him and several other strangers in an attempt to reach the door and exit at the next stop.

'HAHA SORRY FRIEND I HAVE TO GO SUCH A SHAME THAT OUR TOTALLY NORMAL FRIENDSHIP COULD NOT CONTINUE TO BLOSSOM UNDER THESE EXTREMELY SOCIAL CIRCUMSTANCES.'

The bus stranger reaches forward and puts a hand on your shoulder.

'Hey man, no need to—'

You do NOT do well with unplanned physical contact from strangers. You panic and stumble forward, tripping over people.

You reach out for something to hold onto and stabilize yourself but find nothing. Your backpack flies off your shoulder as you fall to the floor. Strangers rush to help you up, and you see one reach for your bag. Before you can tell him to leave it alone, you see the bag's contents tumble out. Three completely raw chickens fall out of your backpack and onto the bus floor. Suddenly, chaos. You sprint to try and grab the chickens in your jaws but now, with all eyes on you, it has become abundantly apparent that you are not a normal commuter. You growl and snap your jaws at what was supposed to be a lovely work lunch, but the chickens continue flopping around the moving bus, gathering more and more filth on their slippery uncooked forms. By this point everyone is screaming but you hope that maybe you can convince them that this is all some sort of misunderstanding. One of the chickens gets within your reach and you bite down on it as hard as you can, spraying chicken liquid over several passengers. The driver looks back in horror, finally having realized the source of the panic, and the bus screeches to a halt. The other chickens slide toward the front of the bus and you run after them, hoping that you can just gather them up and be on your way. However, the commuters are now crowding around you, forcing you toward the front door. The door opens behind you, and you're pushed out into the busy street. Your chickens and backpack are lost to you and your work attire has been horribly soiled. You are attempting to stand back up on two legs when you see the truck coming toward you, moments too late. You're struck.

You lie prone in the street, your suit ruined, your chickens likely blocks away, and your identity compromised. You allow yourself to shed a single tear. You shed a tear not for your imminent death, as

16

all creatures of the forest prepare for the void with each new day, but for the time-sensitive work projects that may never see completion. You shed a tear for the coworkers who may never know what happened to you. You shed a tear for lost opportunities. You shed a tear for the workplace synergy that could have been.

You panicked in a crowded public space and revealed yourself and your chickens. You have faded into the eternal winter. Your story is over.

TODAY IS NOT A GOOD DAY to risk tardiness. It's Friday, and with the weekend so close you would hate for your boss to think that you're actively trying to avoid work. You want to walk through that door right on time, and you're willing to incur an extra expense to do so. You use your phone to pull up Drivr, an app that pairs strangers that can drive with commuters who are willing to pay fourteen dollars for an extra half hour of sleep. You've only used it once, usually opting instead for the crowd-based anonymity of public transit, but today feels special. You give the app your location and watch as it matches you with a driver. The screen beeps as you're paired with Kevin. You see the small car icon that represents Kevin's location nearing your location and you sling your backpack over your shoulder in preparation. However, when you look up, Kevin and his car are nowhere to be seen. You look back down at the screen to see that Kevin has driven straight past you and is now headed in the opposite direction. His car appears to turn around back toward you, but then the little car icon begins spinning in circles two blocks away. The icon then drifts slowly through where, if your memory serves, a bunch of buildings usually are. You're frustrated at how long this is taking but try to cut Kevin some slack because if this small map is any indicator, he's having a really cool time getting to you. Plus, they pay these Drivr drivers, like, nothing.

Eventually, Kevin's Honda Civic rolls up to your location, albeit four minutes behind schedule. You get into the backseat and put your backpack down beside you. The one-on-one setting of this ride would typically make you nervous but ridesharing creates a situation where you sit in the back like some sort of rich person's son while your driver stares straight ahead. You both share awkward small talk and no eye contact. It's a perfect low-stakes social interaction. Kevin smiles, 'Hey, sorry I'm late! This is a new car and I'm still getting the hang of some of the features.'

'OH NO PROBLEM KEVIN I WAS JUST STANDING OUTSIDE LIKE SOME SORT OF ANIMAL HAHA WOULDN'T THAT BE NUTS KEVIN, IF I WAS AN ANIMAL.'

Another perfect save. Kevin pulls out onto the street and speeds the car up. You feel as though maybe he's going a little faster than he should but think that Kevin may just also be concerned about getting you to work on time. Suddenly, the car jerks to a stop. You flop forward a bit and then back, as the car reaches a red light.

'Haha sorry man, I've never driven a stick before. Do you want like a water or something?'

'NO, I THINK I WILL BE OKA—'

Before you can finish, the car slugs forward a little bit before churning fully back into motion. Once again, Kevin is really hitting the gas. You usually don't have trouble in moving vehicles like the bus that move at fairly predictable speeds, but this feels like a different type of ride altogether. With all this commotion, your stomach is starting to churn. You feel all the rotisserie chicken you had for breakfast sloshing around inside of you and attempt to bargain with your own organs to behave for just a few more minutes. The car stops suddenly again, practically throwing you into the front seat.

'Haha sorry about that man, my GPS says there's a quicker way through this alley.'

'OH WOW INCREDIBLE NEWS.'

'Is the music good for you? I can change it to whatever.'

Kevin takes a sharp right turn, pushing and pulling the stick shift seemingly at random, and you realize that you hadn't even heard music. All you can hear now is your heart beating in your ears as you fight with everything you have to keep your breakfast where it's supposed to be. You cannot bring yourself to speak but shake your head vigorously, hoping that Kevin understands that whatever music he is playing has never mattered less. Kevin looks at his GPS and slams on the brakes, forcing your seatbelt hard against your stomach. The car slows almost to a crawl.

'Oh man, that was close. I forgot there's a speed trap up here by the school zone.'

If you could say anything right now, you would apologize to Kevin. But you can't – your mouth is pouring chicken and bile all over Kevin's backseat. You breathe heavily but know that this is just the opening salvo.

'Oh SHIT! Hey man that's not cool—'

'GET ME TO MY OFFICE KEVIN.'

Kevin speeds back up, yanking that goddamn stick every which way again, playing puppeteer with your innards. Each time Kevin hits a stoplight, you find yourself once again spraying a mysterious yellowed liquid all over the back of Kevin's car. You see an entire chicken bone flop onto the floor.

'Listen man, I don't know if you're hungover or what but there's a cleanup fee if you vomit in one of these things,' Kevin says as he turns back toward you.

'KEVIN IF YOU LOOK BACK HERE YOU WILL REGRET IT FOR THE REST OF YOUR LIFE I SWEAR TO YOU ON WHAT-EVER IT IS YOU FIND SACRED IN THIS WORLD I WILL PAY WHATEVER SUM YOU DESIRE JUST GET ME TO MY PLACE OF BUSINESS.'

Kevin's eyes never stray from the road again. He completes your ride without a word of small talk about weather or local sports or even a question about if you like using that rideshare app you clearly just used. He arrives at your office and, wordlessly, you gather up your bag, look at the horrific mess you've created, and thank Mother Nature that you managed to vomit exclusively on Kevin's property, and not on your own clothing. You'd worry about having bad breath, but as someone who mostly eats raw chicken, this is something you've accepted about yourself. Plus, anyone that close to your mouth who cares about the quality of your breath is already dead. You step out of the car and promise yourself not to look back. You look down at your phone to complete the transaction and are given an opportunity to rate Kevin. You give him five stars because you've heard that the ratings heavily influence how much money the Drivr Drivers make, and those guys have it crazy hard.

You made it to the office! Turn to page 24.

BY SOME MIRACLE, you've made it to work with a whole three minutes to spare! You stand on the sidewalk and look up at your office building. The high-rise sits bathed in sun, as though its glass exterior is shining just for you. You take a moment as you do every day to think about how lucky you are to have made it this far. This is a world you were told couldn't be entered. This is a place your kind never thought they should, or even could, see. This is the real uncharted wild.

You step into the building's lobby, make your way into the elevator, and ascend higher into the sky than any wolf dares go. There's a bright ding as the elevator opens and releases you into your business Eden. The office is open and bright, lit only by fluorescent bulbs that look so unlike sunlight that you assume that it must mean they're better somehow. The common space has a wide variety of amenities such as couches, soda machines, and a pool table that you've never seen anyone use but just knowing that the option is out there fills you with excitement. As it turns out, capitalism can make room for *fun*. You are an entry-level graphic designer at this rapidly growing start-up company, and you've earned it. Most humans would've been discouraged by the almost never-ending unpaid internship you endured to get here, but instead you used that time as a chance to observe from a state of near invisibility. The company's exact purpose is still a mystery to you of course, but you've found that very few humans truly understand what their employer does for society. If someone else asks, they just say something like 'that's above my paygrade' and laugh and laugh and laugh. As you walk over toward your desk, you're caught off guard by The Boss, Sharon. You smile and wave, which can make humans a little uneasy, but you always try and avoid any unexpected handshakes. The Boss's suit is much nicer than yours and likely still would be even if yours hadn't been found on the beach. She is a woman of means and presumably gets her clothes from a store and not from the bloated corpse of a businessman who fell off a yacht. You know an interaction with The Boss is rare, so you stand up as tall as you can and try to make eye contact in the business way and not in the way that shows violent intent to other woodland creatures.

'Ah, running a little late today?'

You look at the clock in horror and you feel yourself swell with embarrassment as you realize that the time is now 9:05. You spent so much time marveling at the modern Xanadu that is your workplace that you forgot your contractually obligated work start time of 9:00 a.m. You'll need to deduct this time from your break.

'OH, I AM SO SORRY TRAFFIC WAS JUST A BEAR TODAY.'

Do NOT say bear.

'I MEAN TRAFFIC WAS BAD. I AM A MAN.'

Close call. The Boss clearly sees your embarrassment and benevolently spares you further suffering. 'Hey, hey, no need to get stressed out. We know things happen. Speaking of which, we actually need a handful of people to come in this weekend. We have some folks from corporate in today for a few meetings about our Q4 plans and we'll need to get a jumpstart on roadmapping while they're still in town. You'd be SUCH a rock star if you could help us out . . . '

It's finally happened. You're a rock star. You're a part of the family.

'I WOULD LOVE TO COME IN.' Belinda, the intern who has to come in when you come in, will be THRILLED to hear this. She was sick earlier this week and is likely itching for a chance to prove that she is superhuman and does not need to recover from having limited use of her lungs.

'Incredible, I'll circle back with you at five and we can touch base about what you'll need to do. If I don't see you, we can talk details at Hank's retirement party tonight.'

As quickly as she came, The Boss is gone. She walks quickly away from you on to whatever herculean task business will throw at her next, each step she takes louder and more purposeful than the last. You find that important people walk much louder than everyone else, probably to provoke fear. It works. The Boss is terrifying.

You're slightly embarrassed because you'd forgotten about Hank's retirement party. You don't know Hank well, but in human culture, working at one place for forty years is a tremendous achievement and in wolf culture going forty years without being shot by a bow and arrow is even more impressive, so you want to pay your respects on both levels. However, you've also recently scheduled your very first human date for the exact same time! Eventually, you'll have to decide which matters more to you: your social standing at your $34,500-a-year job or what could very well be your only chance at romantic love. You know that the day ahead of you is going to be a difficult one, but you're prepared to face any challenge.

You get to your desk and place your backpack beneath it for safety. You know better than to trust a communal fridge with your lunch. You catch your coworker Gary shooting you a quick glance as he walks by. You use a standing desk at work because the way your legs and spine connect is different from everyone else and it makes your illusion easier to maintain. This has the added bonus of making you seem somehow more focused on your work, making most of your coworkers less likely to bother you. However, this has never applied to Gary. Gary works just a few desks away and despite being in the sales department, seems to have taken quite an interest in you and your standing desk. As head of sales, he enjoys significantly more financial success than you do. He flaunts this success in the form of a wide variety of suits with terrible colored shirts and ties: a universal sign of confidence. But there is no greater signifier of Gary's middle-management status than his Kia Sportage, or as he will occasionally refer to it, The Garymobile. You find Gary equal parts detestable and fascinating, a man with the confidence of a king, whose only real skill is performing a task frequently and without question. You have yet to figure out if he's the most or least human man you've ever met. He approaches your desk and leans on it with an unearned familiarity, having completely ignored your existence during your intern days until the very moment you received your own desk and dared to stand.

'What's up champ? Rolling in a little late today, got into some Thirsty Thursday trouble last night, huh?'

'ACTUALLY THE TRAFFIC TODAY WAS—'

In an incredible power move, Gary cuts you off. He idly tinkers around with a cup of pens on your desk, a move you recognize. The man may as well be spraying urine to mark his territory.

'Man, I love this desk, dude. So cool, so cool. Y'know, I just was reading this article that said it's actually a little bit better for your back to sit on an exercise ball. It's supposed to help work your core, and we all know you could use a little of that.'

Gary laughs, and playfully punches toward where the abdominal muscles would be on a human torso. He likely expects you to flinch, but you do not. Gary was recently talked to by HR about boundaries and told that if he doesn't learn to respect them, he would only get promoted one or two more times. Three max.

'Anyway, just figured I'd keep you posted in case you wanted to switch over to team exercise ball.'

Gary pauses, seeing if you'll submit to his new and supposedly superior way of sitting all day. You've never been more certain that a minor change to your daily routine could ruin your entire life, so you brush the idea off quickly.

'CALL ME OLD FASHIONED GARY BUT I PREFER TO STAND.'

Gary laughs nervously and knocks on your desk as he starts to walk away.

'Whatever you say champ, but the invitation is wide open.'

When he returns to his desk, he makes direct eye contact with you from across the room as he slowly uses a hand pump to fill his new exercise ball with air before sitting on it. You're fairly certain that you've inadvertently just started a whole thing between you two.

But you don't want to waste any more time worrying about things you can't control. You're sure that whatever childhood deficiency Gary is using this rivalry to process can wait until after you've gotten some work done. It's the morning which means you can either answer the e-mails you received in the eight hours you were too unconscious to look at your phone, or you can head to the kitchen to make coffee and socialize.

If you want to immediately begin wasting corporate time in the name of socialization, turn to page 65.

If you want to read through your e-mails, turn to page 74.

AS YOUR EYES HIT the treeline, you feel the slow realization of the truth spreading across your whole body. You swear that the sound of the wind blowing through the trees is calling to you. Not in words, but with a panoply of scents carrying the singular reminder of a long-lost home. Your mistakes have driven you back to where it all began. You should feel ashamed of this, but you don't care anymore. You fire forward like a celestial object hurtling into the unknown. With each bounding leap forward your suit tears more and more, and as you reach the trees, you feel it fly off your back.

You are free, beautiful, and as fearsome as you've ever been. You're a wolf once more and you're never looking back. You spring through the trees until you can't see, hear, or smell even the smallest trace of humanity. You sprint for what feels like a lifetime, but you never feel tired. Suddenly, you hear something you haven't heard in a very long time: your name.

You stop suddenly, scanning the forest around you. But you never see him coming. You're struck from the side and knocked to the ground. You snarl in confusion at first, but you'd know this scent anywhere. This is your brother. He speaks to you in the elegant language of the wolves.

'AND LO, THE PRODIGAL SON RETURNS,' your brother says, laughing. The prodigal son to which he refers is a wolf version of that one Bible story about a young man that leaves his family behind to live a non-traditional life. You were very surprised when you found out humans had that story too. It's an extremely convenient allegory for your situation.

'I HAVE COME HOME BROTHER. I AM SO SORRY FOR LEAVING. MY GRAND DALLIANCE WAS ALL FOR NOUGHT.'

Your brother looks at the ground, pained by the memory of your departure.

'I HAD THOUGHT AS MUCH BUT IN THIS WOOD EACH MUST FIND THEIR OWN WAY.'

Wolves are not sentimental creatures, but they value family above all else. You know that your decisions affected your brother greatly, especially after losing your family to the great mini-mall purge of 2013, but what matters now is that the two of you are together again.

31

'IT WOULD SEEM THAT FATE HAS CONSPIRED TO RETURN YOU TO US AT THE PERFECT TIME. OUR GRAND DESIGN NEARS COMPLETION.'

Your brother sees the clear confusion on your face and gestures for you to follow him.

'I DO NOT BLAME YOU FOR LEAVING US BEHIND BROTHER. HUMANITY HAS TAKEN SO MUCH.'

The two of you walk up a hill that you know you've seen before, perhaps sometime in your youth.

'YOU SEE BROTHER, THE WHOLE FOREST HAS GROWN TIRED OF HUMANITY'S REPEATED INDIGNITIES. IT IS TIME. WE ARE TAKING IT ALL BACK.'

You know you've been here before.

'TAKING WHAT BACK? BROTHER WHERE ARE YOU TAKING ME?'

'HOME.'

The two of you reach the top of the hill and find yourselves overlooking an unmistakable landscape. The land below is where you were born. The very same place from which your family was displaced when it was foolishly turned into a mini-mall long after mini-malls started to be widely considered to be terrible investments. And now it stood, mostly abandoned. Barely worth what it cost.

'THE MINI-MALL?'

'IT STRUGGLES BROTHER. IT STANDS HARDLY GUARDED, WITH NOTHING BUT A FAILING VIDEO RENTAL STORE. AND AT DAWN, IT WILL BE OURS.'

'BUT HOW? MINI-MALLS HAVE SURVIVED THIS LONG, THEY ARE NOT TO BE UNDERESTIMATED.'

32

Your brother looks at you knowingly, 'YOUR RETURN WILL NOT GO UNNOTICED BROTHER. I BELIEVE THAT YOU CAN CONVINCE THE CREATURES OF THE FOREST TO FIGHT ALONGSIDE US.'

You're surprised at this news. You've been an entry-level corporate employee for so long that you had forgotten that you're the King of Wolves. You feel very silly for a moment before giving your brother a solemn nod. You'll need a lot of help to win, and you only have a day to gather your forces. The politics of the forest are complicated. Rivalries are centuries old, sometimes with origins that have been lost to time. This will require rebuilding bridges that burned long ago. Maybe your time in the human world will help you bring stability to the natural one. Or maybe it's pushed you further away from your fellow beasts than you ever were before. You know there's no hope of victory in this fight without the brute force of bears.

As you make your way into the hills the bears call home, you hear a low rumbling in the brush next to you. You and your brother pace forward, keeping your eyes ahead as you approach a moss-covered cave. Bears emerge from the brush and begin walking alongside you. You're quickly outnumbered, but the two of you aren't so foolish as to be intimidated. You've come to speak to the Queen of Bears, and you won't be deterred. You pause in front of a nearby cave and wait. The Queen lumbers out of her cave and roars in a display of power.

'WHAT BRINGS WOLVES TO MY HOME?'

You'll need to choose your words carefully. The Queen will hear

33

you out, but bears aren't known for their patience. You cut to the chase.

'MY BROTHER AND I WISH TO LEAD AN ATTACK ON THE HUMANS. WE WISH TO RECLAIM WHAT IS OURS. WE WISH TO CONQUER THE FINAL VIDEO RENTAL STORE.'

The Queen lets out a hearty laugh, a sound that would terrify most lesser creatures. You can already see her growing annoyed with you. Bears and wolves have maintained peace for a long time, but it's a fragile one. As two apex predators, you've found that the only way to coexist has been to stay out of each other's way. If you want their help, you'll need to be convincing. How do you plan to convince the Queen to lend you her aid?

To offer a piece of wartime wisdom, turn to page 35.

To offer a flattering compliment, turn to page 37.

34

YOU DON'T BECOME the ruler of all bears without good instincts. The Queen is a wise leader. You need to appeal to her strategic mind.

'YOU ARE NOT WRONG TO BE SKEPTICAL. BUT REMEMBER QUEEN THAT THE HUMANS HAVE TAKEN JUST AS MUCH FROM YOU AS THEY HAVE FROM US. AND AS THEY SAY, THE ENEMY OF MY ENEMY IS MY FRIEND.'

The Queen processes this for a moment. She appears to be deep in thought.

Then one of the other bears interjects, 'WHO SAYS THAT?'

Oh no.

'DIDN'T A HUMAN SAY THAT?'

Yikes. This other bear knows his stuff.

'I AM LIKE ONE HUNDRED PER CENT SURE THAT A HUMAN SAID THAT ORIGINALLY.'

The bears begin to advance upon you. This is very bad.

'IS THIS TRUE?' bellows The Queen. 'DID YOU JUST QUOTE A HUMAN THING?'

Another bear chimes in, aggressively approaching the first bear.

'WAIT. HOW DID YOU KNOW THAT HUMANS SAID THAT?'

The first bear nervously looks back and forth before attempting to run. The situation implodes. Bears turn on other bears, convinced of traitors within their ranks, and the Queen is suddenly upon you. You and your brother are pulled into the melee, and in the coming hours the whole forest quickly returns to its chaotic natural state as it's swallowed by civil war.

You tried to say something cool and instead accidentally brought a centuries-old peace to an end. The woods have fallen into chaos and your war is finished before it begins. Your story is over.

YOU KNOW FULL WELL that the only true currency in the woods is your word. If the Queen is to be expected to help you in your hour of need, she must know that you believe in her and in her species' strength.

'I UNDERSTAND YOUR SKEPTICISM. ONE SO STRONG AS YOURSELF HAS NO OBLIGATION TO ANYONE.'

The Queen seems flattered.

'OH, WOW YOU THINK WE ARE STRONG?'

'OF COURSE. YOU ALL ARE SO BIG.'

'THAT IS SUPER NICE OF YOU HONESTLY I WAS TOTALLY HAVING ONE OF THOSE DAYS WHERE I WAS JUST LIKE WOW WHAT AM I EVEN DOING SO I REALLY APPRECIATE YOU SAYING THAT.'

'NO PROBLEM WE ALL HAVE THOSE DAYS AND FOR REAL YOU ALL SHOULD BE REALLY PROUD OF YOUR-SELVES.'

The Queen's mood has clearly improved; you can tell she had been really stressed out and it feels nice to have helped her relax. She approaches you and your brother and stands upright.

'THANK YOU FOR BEING A VERY EMPOWERING FRIEND. WE WILL AID YOU IN THE WAR TO COME.'

The Queen lets out a horrific roar, which is actually very nice in bear culture. Once again, the power of common decency has brought order to the animal world. You've gathered a strong force, but your army must grow even larger if you want to stand any sort of chance. You have the most ferocious animals in all the land on your side, but now you need to turn your attention to the skies. The Lord of All Birds will see it as a personal insult if you don't invite birds to your big war. With a force that big, the mini-mall will be yours in no time. But the Lord of All Birds is not charitable. He will expect something in return. You and your brother make your way to a wooded glen that the Lord of All Birds calls his home. You can't see any birds, but you hear rustling from above. You're being watched.

'LORD OF ALL BIRDS. I KNOW YOU ARE WATCHING RIGHT NOW AND I ASK THAT YOU GRANT ME AN AUDI-ENCE. THE WOLVES AND BEARS HAVE FORMED AN ALLIANCE AND WE PLAN TO TAKE BACK SOME OF OUR LAND FROM HUMAN CONTROL. ALSO, I AM BACK, HOW ARE YOU?'

The trees fall silent. You can just barely hear the wind softly moving the branches. It's a beautiful day, you're almost sad to be spending it planning a war. You hear a piercing cry from above and suddenly you sense movement all around you. From the canopies above shoot hundreds of birds of all shapes and sizes. They fly around you and your brother erratically – you're almost convinced that they mean to attack. But then, the Lord of All Birds emerges.

He lands on a branch across from you and his subjects all land as well, listening attentively.

'I NEVER THOUGHT I'D SEE YOU AGAIN, KING OF WOLVES.'

You keep forgetting you're a king. It's good to be back.

'I HAVE SURPRISED MANY TODAY, BUT I COULD NOT STOMACH LIVING AMONGST THE HUMANS. THEY ARE A VILE, DECADENT PEOPLE WHO DO NOT CLEAN UP THEIR DISHES FROM COMMUNAL SPACES.'

The Lord of All Birds nods solemnly.

'WE ARE ALL ALLOWED OUR LAPSES IN JUDGMENT. YOUR PEOPLE WILL BE GLAD TO HAVE YOU BACK.'

'THANK YOU, I ONLY HOPE THAT YOU WILL JOIN US IN OUR GREAT FIGHT.'

'I AM SURE YOUR CAUSE IS NOBLE. HOWEVER, THE BIRDS ARE NOT ENTIRELY SURE WE HAVE THE EMOTIONAL BANDWIDTH FOR A WAR RIGHT NOW. WE HAVE A LOT GOING ON, HONESTLY.'

You were worried about this. The Lord of All Birds is very dramatic and seems to always be in the midst of some sort of personal distress. At first you thought you just met him during a dramatic time in his life but eventually you realized that he's just always like this. He pretends to be all vague about it but really, he cannot wait until you ask to know more. But you know him. You won't take the bait.

'I ASSURE YOU LORD, THIS BATTLE IS MORE IMPORT-ANT THAN ANY MERE PERSONAL SQUABBLE.'

'IT'S JUST THIS WHOLE THING WITH MY EX, OUR RELA-TIONSHIP GOT VERY TOXIC TOWARD THE END AND—'

You cut him off, already bored. Your brother shoots you a look and rolls his eyes. This guy is such a piece of work.

'THERE WILL BE NO LAND LEFT FOR OVERLY COMPLI-CATED RELATIONSHIPS THAT SHOULD HAVE ENDED SIX MONTHS AGO IF WE DO NOT PUT A STOP TO HUMAN EXPANSION. NOW THIS FIRST STRIKE WILL LET THEM KNOW THAT WE DO NOT PLAN TO GO QUIETLY.'

The Lord of All Birds seems shocked and a little hurt. This may not have been the best play, but you don't have the luxury of time to think it over right now.

'I SEE HOW IT IS.'

'OH LORD I'M SORRY.'

'NO, I GET IT. SERIOUSLY. IT'S FINE. I'M NOT MAD.'

There's an awkward silence. The Lord of All Birds is for sure mad. You feel a little bad for calling out his mess of a personal life in front of everyone. You're sure he's trying his best. If you really want to insult a leader to his face and still get what you want, you'll have to offer up something that will really get his attention. You break the tension.

'WHAT IF WE HELPED YOU BROKER A TRUCE WITH THE INSECTS? THAT SEEMS LIKE SOMETHING AN EX WOULD FIND IMPRESSIVE.'

This is a risky choice. Nobody likes dealing with the insects. They function as a hive mind so you're technically talking to thou-sands of them at any given time but you're also only talking to one of them. It's tough to understand and even tougher to develop any sort of personal relationship. For the most part, the rest of the woods leave them alone because they're super important to the ecosystem, but tons of birds use them as food. It's awkward.

'THIS . . . ' He trails off, intrigued. 'THIS COULD WORK FOR US. THE INSECTS DO NOT NEED TO JOIN US, BUT THEY MUST AGREE TO A TRUCE DURING OUR FIGHT. IF YOU CAN MAKE THAT HAPPEN THEN THE BIRDS SHALL JOIN YOU AT THE FRONT LINE.'

The insects are a hard sell but on the other hand you've nearly convinced two leaders to go to war today, so how hard can it be to convince a third to enjoy peace? There's no time to consider other options.

———

Turn to page 42.

THE GROUND GROWS DAMP and reeks of stagnant water as you approach the forested swamp that the insects call home. The air is so thick with humidity that your whole body feels as though it's already been submerged in the muck. Your brother turns to you with a nervousness about him that you aren't used to seeing.

'ARE YOU SURE ABOUT THIS? THE COLONY OF INSECTS IS NOTORIOUSLY UNPREDICTABLE. HOW CAN WE TRUST THEM?'

'WE CAN'T TRUST THEM, BUT WE DON'T HAVE TO. WE JUST NEED THE LORD OF ALL BIRDS ON OUR SIDE. IF HE'S WILLING TO TRUST THE COLONY, THEN THAT'S HIS MISTAKE. NOW HUSH, WE'RE APPROACHING. WE DO NOT WANT TO BE OVERHEARD.'

You reach the swamp's edge and begin to hear the low hum of insects gathering around you. Their voices come from all around you to form one unified, deeply unsettling voice. It would sound melodic if it weren't underlined by the frenetic buzzing of thousands of bugs.

'*Ah if it isn't the Brothers Wolf. It has been a long time. A long time indeed.*'

The Brothers Wolf is not something you and your brother call yourselves. You really hope that they aren't telling people you call yourselves that.

'HELLO, COLONY. I APOLOGIZE FOR OUR ABSENCE. WE ARE NOT BUILT FOR THE SWAMPS AS YOU ARE.'

'*Are you calling us gross?*'

'WHAT? NO, NO I WOULD NEVER—'

'*Sorry it's just that everyone thinks swamps are gross and you just said that we were built for them so it just kind of threw us for a second there. Wolves aren't so great either you know. Everyone talks about how bizarre it is that you pee on things to claim them.*'

'OH NO I WAS NOT TRYING TO INSULT YOU, IT'S JUST WET HERE. BUT NOW I FEEL LIKE YOU'VE INSULTED ME?'

The insects make a horrible noise that you can only assume is some sort of laugh.

'*Relax friend, we're just kidding around.*'

It didn't really sound like the insects were kidding around but luckily, months of experience in Corporate America have trained you in the art of learning to work with someone who is actively gaslighting you.

'WELL AT ANY RATE I AM SORRY. I COME TO YOU TODAY TO DISCUSS A MATTER OF UTMOST IMPORTANCE.'

'*We know what you've come to discuss. You wish to start a war and hope to receive assurances from us. Wherever there is one of us, we are there. Listening.*'

43

'SO YOU KNOW THE IMPORTANCE OF OUR FIGHT. WE DO NOT REQUIRE THAT YOU JOIN US, ONLY THAT YOU AGREE TO LEAVE THE SKIES PEACEFUL WHILE WE ARE IN THE THROES OF BATTLE.'

'*And what gives you, Brothers Wolf, the authority to command us? You come on behalf of the birds, who consume so many of us. You come on the heels of your personal sabbatical to the human world. What gives you any right to start such a frivolous war?*'

Anger takes root in your entire body. You cannot believe the audacity of these bugs. In one breath they have insulted your process of marking territory, your time in the human world, and the validity of your war. You're consumed with the desire to finally tell the bugs exactly what you think of them. They've had it too good for too long. But also, you're here representing many others. It may be in your best interest to behave like a diplomat.

If you choose to really let them know how you feel, turn to page 45.

If you choose to try and resolve their questions in a more diplomatic way, turn to page 47.

'OKAY, THAT'S IT. I'VE HAD IT. I AM ALL OUT OF PATIENCE.'

You cannot stand these guys and you're frankly sick of pretending they're anything other than an ecologically necessary annoyance.

'Oh yeah you've been here a full five minutes, must have been agony. God you are a real piece of work, you know that right?'

'OH, SHUT UP. I AM DONE WITH YOU. I COME HERE OFFERING YOU ALL A DEAL, MAKING MYSELF VULNER- ABLE, TRYING TO START A BIG WAR, AND YOU IMMEDI- ATELY INSULT ME. THEN ON TOP OF IT ALL, YOU KEEP CALLING MY BROTHER AND ME "THE BROTHERS WOLF" LIKE THAT'S A THING. IT'S NOT A THING, THAT'S A SUPER BIZARRE THING TO CALL US. IF YOU WANT TO CALL HIM ANYTHING, CALL HIM KYLE, THAT'S HIS NAME. BUT YOU HAD TO PICK THE WEIRDEST POSSIBLE WAY TO GREET US, IT'S LIKE YOU PRIDE YOURSELF ON MAKING INTER- ACTIONS WITH YOU DIFFICULT. I DO NOT KNOW HOW YOU MANAGE TO STAY SANE SITTING ALONE WITH HUNDREDS OF THOUSANDS OF YOURSELF. YOU ARE SO WEIRD. EVERYONE TALKS ABOUT IT.'

You were full-throated yelling there. You look around and see your brother, horrified at your little outburst. Wolves are typically restrained. Maybe your time with the humans *did* change you. You may have just ended your life. Though if you did, you picked a cathartic way to go.

'OH MAN, I'M SORRY. THAT WAS A LOT.'

'*No, no. I get it. You know, not a lot of creatures come through here and if they do, they always want something. You're no different. But you are the first one to be honest with me and for that you have my respect. For that, you'll have your peace.*'

You take a deep breath and sigh. You're in shock that this went your way and you're doubly in shock to learn that insects place such a high value on the concept of respect. But you don't dwell on it long.

'WE MAY HAVE OUR DIFFERENCES, BUT I APPRECIATE YOUR SUPPORT. YOU WILL NOT REGRET IT.'

You leave the swamp just as the sun begins to set. You'll have the night to prepare but at dawn, you start a war.

———

Turn to page 50.

'WE UNDERSTAND THAT THIS IS NOT YOUR FIGHT. BUT WE ALSO KNOW THAT YOU KNOW WHAT IT IS TO STAND UP TO YOUR PREDATORS. SENDING A MESSAGE TO THE HUMANS THAT WE CANNOT BE CONQUERED IS IMPORT-ANT. THEY MUST KNOW THAT THEIR RULE IS MORE TENUOUS THAN THEY BELIEVE.'

'You cannot win us over to your side with posturing. We see what you truly desire.'

'WHAT DO YOU MEAN?'

'As always, we know more than you think we do. We're aware that the land you wish to reclaim was the place you were raised. You wish to bring us all into a war for your own nostalgia.'

The insects swarm around you, giving you and your brother no room to breathe.

'You gamble with our lives to settle your petty score.'

This insult to the significance of your land makes your brother furious. He breaks composure.

'YOU EXPECT US TO BE IMPRESSED WITH YOUR EAVES-DROPPING? YOU EXPECT US TO BE INTIMIDATED BY

YOUR INCESSANT BUZZING AS YOU PRATTLE ON? YOU ARE NO LEADER AND NO WARRIOR. WE ARE LEAVING. COME BROTHER, WE WILL FIND ANOTHER WAY TO BROKER THIS ALLIANCE.'

You see what's about to happen but can't say anything in time. Your brother steps forward to leave and inadvertently squishes several of the encroaching bugs underfoot. The hive moves on him immediately.

'First you attempt to manipulate us and now you bring violence to our home?'

'LET HIM GO!' you scream, but they won't. You see your brother lifted off the ground by thousands of bugs. You expect to hear him cry out in pain but instead he's consumed until you cannot see him. One by one, his bones fall to the ground, picked clean. You feel yourself frothing into a feral rage.

'HOLY SHIT.'

'Oh my God, I'm sorry, I didn't mean to do that.'

'YOU ABSOLUTELY DID, YOU SON OF A BITCH. YOU CONTROL ALL THESE INSECTS, DON'T YOU?'

'Okay yes but I was mad. Wow that was so violent, I'm sorry, I guess I just got caught up in the drama.'

You start squishing every bug you can but it's no good. They're on you just as they were on your brother. You feel a brief, horrific pain all over your body and then – nothing.

Wow! Everything went really poorly with the bugs. Things got so out of hand that you and your brother got murdered. Your story is over.

YOUR FORCES GATHER on the hilltop as the first hint of dawn starts to pour over the horizon. You stand alongside your brother, the Queen of Bears, and the Lord of All Birds in silence. As the light grows, you look back onto your forces. Wolves, bears, and birds are joined side-by-side. Even some of the boring animals are there too, like deer and lizards and you're pretty sure you saw some sort of wild pig. You have an army and a target; all that's left is to give the order. It's all come to this. After nearly twenty-four hours of dreaming of this moment, you're about to take back the land on which you were raised.

'THIS WAS YOUR IDEA, WOLVES. I BELIEVE YOU MAY HAVE THE HONOR OF BEGINNING THE WAR.'

That's really nice of the Queen of Bears; usually that honor goes to the largest creature. She's so great once you get to know her. You make mental note of that. You address your army.

'CREATURES OF THE FOREST. THE HUMANS HAVE TAKEN SO MUCH FROM US. OUR FOOD IS TAKEN FROM US TO MAKE THEIRS. OUR HOMES ARE BULLDOZED

TO BUILD THEIRS. THE GRAVES OF OUR FOREFATHERS BECOME THE FOUNDATIONS OF THEIR SBARROS.'

'WHAT IS SBARROS?' You hear the question come from the back, but decide to breeze right past that because then you'll have to explain the concept of pizza and that's actually one of the only things humans have done right.

'IT DOES NOT MATTER, IT'S BAD.'

'SORRY.' Okay this guy's heart is in the right place apologizing, but interrupting to apologize for interrupting really defeats the purpose of apologizing in the first place.

'OKAY WHATEVER. ANYWAY, WE ARE GOING TO RETAKE THIS MINI-MALL TODAY. THIS SMALL FIRST RECLAMATION OF LAND WILL LET THE HUMANS KNOW THAT NATURE AND ITS CREATURES ARE NOT SO EASILY CAST ASIDE.'

The first crescent of sun falls over the land and finally hits the hill, bathing your army in the glorious light of war.

'TO BATTLE, CHILDREN OF THE FOREST!'

You break past the treeline with the other leaders, followed by the most incredible army the woods have ever seen. As you cascade down the hill, you try to see what forces the humans have amassed to defend themselves, but as you reach the mini-mall, you see that there are none. Instead you see a parking lot that's empty except for one car. In it, there's a terrified young woman filming the whole spectacle with her phone. Her uniform matches the color scheme of the video rental store behind you. You wanted a battle for the soul of the forest, but this isn't it. This woman is innocent. She's just on her way to work like you were not so long ago.

'WHAT ARE YOU WAITING FOR BROTHER? THERE IS ONLY ONE HUMAN HERE. WE SHOULD DISPENSE WITH HER AND CELEBRATE OUR GOOD FORTUNE.'

You're the King of Wolves. You should have no problem doing what needs to be done to win this fight. But you were never very good at being a wolf. The part of you that understands humans would never eat someone, especially not someone who'd done nothing to wrong you. But didn't you leave that part of you behind? Are all humans not guilty for what mini-malls have done to your people's home?

'BROTHER IF WE KILL THIS GIRL, WE ARE NO BETTER THAN THE HUMANS. WE SHOULD ATTEMPT TO TALK TO HER.'

You approach the car and gesture downward at your captive with your head. She looks at you, stunned at your attempt to communicate but compliant. She rolls the window down just enough to speak. As the only creature capable of communicating in both languages, you step forward from the crowd.

'HELLO. WE ARE SORRY TO DISTURB YOU BUT THE CREATURES OF THE FOREST HAVE DECIDED TO RECLAIM THE LAND THAT IS RIGHTFULLY—'

'Take whatever you want! Please, I just manage the Tapes of Wrath, the video store down there. All the other stores are out of business. I don't know what the hell is happening here but please just let me go home!'

This is going to be a bummer to explain to the gang, who have all gotten pretty psyched up for a big war. It seems like the American economy killed this mini-mall long before you even raised your army. Just as you begin to think about ways to break this to everyone, another car pulls into the parking lot and a man gets out. He walks through your army with an incredible confidence, oblivious to what was going on before he arrived. He comes up to the window and addresses the young woman.

'Hey Sam, you open up the shop yet? I was hoping to pick up a few things before I headed into work.'

Seriously, this guy seems completely oblivious to the incredible variety of woodland creatures you've assembled. She stares at him in horror and gestures frantically toward your army.

'Randy! Get help!'

Randy looks around as though he just entered the same dimension as you.

'Woah, wild. Well, I get you're doing a thing, but if I could hop in the shop real quick, I could just grab a copy of *Porpoise Nights* and be on my way.'

Randy is giving off an absolutely serene energy. He smells like your roommate smelled sometimes when he said he was writing but was actually just eating clementines on the couch. If the circumstances were different, you could learn a lot from Randy's seemingly boundless calm. But unfortunately, you're at war. Randy may have just given you the solution to your army's unquenched bloodlust that you needed. You could easily make an example of him and still keep your army from eating the woman in the car. But perhaps there's some way you could spare them both.

––––––––––

If you try to spare both Randy and Sam, turn to page 56.

If you sacrifice Randy, turn to page 63.

IT MAY BE TEMPTING to indulge in the bloodbath you'd all imagined when this war started, but you know in your heart that neither Randy nor Sam have been a driving force in the injustices done to you.

You address your eagerly awaiting brethren: 'FELLOW CREATURES, THESE TWO HUMANS ARE NOT SPECIAL. THEY DID NOT TURN THIS LAND INTO A MINI-MALL. THEY CANNOT TURN IT BACK. THEY ARE SIMPLY A SMALL, UNWITTING PART OF A MUCH LARGER VIRUS. THE MEN THAT CAUSED THIS ARE FAR AWAY, IN WARM HOMES WITH FULL BELLIES. TO FEAST UPON THESE TWO AND CALL IT VICTORY WOULD BE TO LIE TO OURSELVES. INSTEAD, I DECREE THAT WE SHALL LET THEM GO. IF WE MAKE OUR POINT WITHOUT HURTING OR EVEN INCONVENIENCING ANYONE, PERHAPS THE HUMANS WILL UNDERSTAND THE NOBILITY OF OUR PLIGHT AND STRIKE A DEAL WITH US. AND IF NOT, THE WAR CONTINUES ON.'

There are groans from the crowd, but you'll deal with dissenters later. You've still taken back the land. You address Randy and Sam.

'YOU TWO MUST GO. TELL YOUR FRIENDS AND FAMILY WHAT YOU WITNESSED TODAY AND LET THEM KNOW THAT THIS MINI-MALL IS ONCE AGAIN THE PROPERTY OF THE CREATURES OF THE FOREST.'

Randy looks at you, puzzled.

'Can I . . . still grab my tape?'

This man has the self-assurance of a young god.

'UM SURE, YOU CAN TAKE YOUR BELONGINGS BUT ONCE YOU HAVE DONE THAT YOU MUST BE GONE FROM THIS LAND.'

Randy walks into the store and you follow him. He grabs a tape from the rack and reaches for his wallet.

'THERE IS NO NEED FOR THAT, MONEY IS NO GOOD HERE ANYMORE.'

'I'm not gonna get Sam in trouble man, jeez.'

'OKAY GOOD POINT, LEAVE THE MONEY SO THAT CAN BE TAKEN CARE OF AND THEN BE GONE FROM THIS PLACE ONCE AND FOR ALL.'

Randy returns to his car. Sam looks at you, seeming puzzled at the fact that she's actually made it out of this alive.

'The money in the register needs to get to the bank before close. My next shift is Wednesday, I'll see you then, I guess.'

'WAIT WHAT?'

Sam's car shudders to life and you gesture to the other animals to make room. She peels out of the parking lot.

'WE'VE DONE IT EVERYONE. THIS MINI-MALL BELONGS TO THE CREATURES OF THE FOREST ONCE AGAIN.'

After a moment of confusion, there are cheers. Despite the battle not quite being what they'd expected, it would appear that everyone is thrilled to have won. Another car slowly pulls into the parking lot. A young couple and their child exit.

'Hey, is the store open yet?'

Okay wow, well if you didn't eat Randy you cannot eat this family.

'LET ME SEE WHAT WE CAN DO.'

———

Turn to page 59.

ONE YEAR LATER

HORSE'S ASS, your brother is late again. According to the sign-in sheet on the staff board, he was supposed to start his shift twenty minutes ago. You've been managing Tapes of Wrath ever since Sam went off to college. As it turns out, when she told everyone she could that woodland creatures had claimed ownership of a local video store, it drew a crowd rather than inspiring fear. What started as politely trying to get people the tapes they wanted so that you wouldn't have to eat anybody, spiraled out of control when some of the birds started demanding compensation for their time. Before you knew it, you were turning a modest profit. It's not what anyone expected, but you figure that something that keeps everyone busy can't be that bad. You stand at the door waiting impatiently when your brother sheepishly approaches, quickly trying to put on his work vest.

'SORRY BROTHER, I OVERSLEPT.'

'I DO NOT WANT TO HEAR IT.'

'I'M SERIOUS, I'VE BEEN FEELING SICK, I NEEDED THE REST.'

'WELL IT'S COMING OUT OF YOUR PAYCHECK. I CANNOT COVER FOR YOU ANYMORE. IT LOOKS BAD WHEN I TREAT YOU DIFFERENTLY. THE QUEEN OF BEARS HAD TO STAY LATE COVERING CHECKOUT FOR YOU. DO YOU THINK THAT WAS FUN FOR ME TO ASK HER TO DO? DO YOU THINK THAT WAS A FUN THING TO ASK OF A QUEEN?'

'WELL I WOULDN'T BE SICK SO OFTEN IF I HAD HEALTH INSURANCE.'

'OH, DO NOT START WITH ME ON THIS AGAIN, CORPOR- ATE ONLY GIVES HEALTH INSURANCE TO FULL-TIME EMPLOYEES AND YOU ARE NOT FULL-TIME.'

'BROTHER, I WORK THIRTY-EIGHT HOURS A WEEK. DO YOU THINK THAT'S A COINCIDENCE?'

'HEY WE PAY YOU, DON'T WE? ARE YOU NOT HAPPY HERE? BECAUSE THERE ARE HUNDREDS OF ANIMALS OUTSIDE LIVING IN ABSOLUTE, UNFETTERED FREEDOM THAT I'M SURE WOULD TAKE THIS JOB IN A HEARTBEAT.'

'EAT SHIT BROTHER, I MEAN THAT. THIS PLACE IS A GODDAMN PRISON.'

Your brother storms off to go start his shift and you let out a long, exhausted sigh before going over to sort the return bin.

———

Whoops! You accidentally introduced capitalism to the natural world, and it spread like a virus. Instead of reclaim- ing what was yours, you now manage a semi-successful

video store with somewhat exploitative compensation practices. Happens to the best of us.

THE END.

YOU WISH WITH ALL YOUR HEART that this war could end without claiming the lives of innocents, but your army thirsts for blood. If not Randy's, it's likely to be yours.

'LET THIS MAN SERVE AS A MESSAGE TO MANKIND. THIS PLACE IS OURS.'

You gesture to the Queen of Bears and the Lord of All Birds.

'IN EXCHANGE FOR YOUR AID, I OFFER YOU TWO THIS RANDY AS TRIBUTE.'

Randy gazes upon the Queen of Bears as she looms over him.

'Woah, that dog is huge!'

Suddenly she grabs hold of him and the Lord of All Birds grabs him from the other side. Before you know what's going on, he has been pulled in half, spraying blood everywhere. The animals lucky enough to be close to the carcass immediately begin feasting on his flesh and bone. You totally forgot how bears eat. It's a mess. Trying to look away from the carnage, you gesture to Sam, still cowering in her car. You figure a quick apology won't hurt since no one else speaks human.

'LEAVE THIS PLACE AND NEVER RETURN. FORGET ALL THAT YOU'VE SEEN HERE. ALSO I AM REALLY SORRY YOU HAD TO SEE THAT.'

As her car vanishes into the distance, you and your army look upon the land you've claimed. In the morning air, it seems impossibly still. It's nearly silent, with only the sounds of leaves in the trees and bears slowly eating Randy. You've taken back what's yours, but you can't tell if it's peaceful or desolate. You stare at it, sharing a moment of reflection with your brother.

'BROTHER PERHAPS WE WERE WRONG. PERHAPS THERE'S NOTHING LEFT TO RECLAIM HERE. WHAT THEY TOOK IS GONE. OUR HOME WAS DEAD THE MOMENT THEY BUILT THIS MONSTROSITY. ALL WE SUCCEEDED IN DOING TODAY WAS RECLAIMING ITS SUN-BLEACHED BONES. ARE WE DOOMED TO REPEAT THIS CYCLE FOREVER? ARE WE MORE THAN THE VIOLENCE WE VISIT UPON EACH OTHER? OR ARE WE TRAPPED BY OUR OWN TRAGICALLY SIMPLE BIOLOGY?'

You hear a muffled noise behind you. You turn to see your brother trying to respond through a mouth full of Randy.

'SORRY I DIDN'T CATCH THAT. DID YOU WANT SOME OF THIS BECAUSE WE'RE RUNNING OUT FAST?'

Congratulations! You stole back a mini-mall that used to be a beautiful forest and in the process began to question the violent nature of both human society and your own. Also, Randy died. Your story ends here.

WHILE IT ALWAYS FELT counterintuitive to you to take a break before doing any actual work, you've found that humans hate the morning so much that accomplishing anything within those first few hours of the day is seen as cause for celebration. A trip to the employee kitchen is a common reward for someone who just completed a brief and simplistic task. Plus, office work is a war fought on many fronts, the most important of which is a social one. For you this isn't just a relaxing way to kill time. This is your proving ground.

You head toward the kitchen to fraternize. The lounge has just one coffee machine to sustain an entire staff, so half the fun of the kitchen seems to be that people get to wait in a very long line for access to the beverage that makes waking up in the morning seem like a good idea. But you don't need that beverage. You mostly don't need it because the one time you drank it you could only think about murder and your own heartbeat for three hours. But also, you don't drink it because you don't need to. Coffee is a way for humans to forget their distaste for the routine, but for you that's the appeal. Your options are the repetitive drudgery of entry-level office work or an uncaring wilderness where nobody dies of old age. Death out there involves getting ripped in half. Here, death is more of a slow, metaphorical experience. If you do it right, you barely feel a thing. You figure it's a matter of preference.

You plod into the staff lounge and see a regrettably slim selection of coworkers. The Boss has entered a high-profile meeting, leaving the office without the watchful eye of its highest-ranking supervisor. You'd assumed that this would've sent a veritable who's who of high-value coworkers into the open but unfortunately, it's just Mike. But there's no turning back now. In an office it's important to pretend to love everyone entirely more than they have earned, but also equally. You have been told time and time again that this is a family, which you appreciate, but even with your limited experience you know that not every family is cursed with a Mike. Instead of seeing a situation where two near-strangers are forced to stand in a shared space together for a few minutes, Mike sees an opportunity to make small talk. He's a difficult man to describe, as he seems to have been solely engineered to be both well-meaning and devoid of any interesting traits.

'Heyyyy man, Happy Friday!'

There are nights where you lay awake wondering if any of this was a good idea. You wonder if maybe you're more out of place here than you ever were in the woods. You get incredibly lonely on those nights, feeling like the idea of a place to call home might have just been a lie someone told you to help you forget how cold it gets at night. You wonder if maybe those feelings could be staved off by the addition of just one good friend. That friend will never be Mike. Good lord, you hope that friend will not be Mike.

Oh God, the entire time you've been thinking about how apocalyptically boring Mike is, he's been talking. Worse yet, he's pulled out some kind of greeting card.

In the course of any given week, you are prompted to sign at least one card. The vast majority of the time, they're celebrating someone's birthday but in rare cases, the card is because someone received even better news than the continued advancement of their age. This news usually involved a promotion or sometimes even a move to a new city. The sentiments, while incredibly similar merit different personalized well-wishes in the card signature below. Without having heard the card's purpose, you're congratulating blind.

'Anyway, I figured I could get it to Tamara during lunch so if you wanted to sign first, you can save me the trouble of tracking you down in an hour!'

Of course, no one else has signed yet. You're staring at a blank card here with moments to make a decision that will be sure to set the tone of Tamara's entire birthday/other celebration. Mike holds out a pen. You have to make your decision quickly: will you simply wish Tamara a happy birthday? Or will you try to say something more generally congratulatory at the risk of sounding slightly out of context?

———

If you sign 'Happy Birthday', turn to page 68.

If you opt for something more general, turn to page 70.

YOU CAREFULLY GRAB THE PEN from Mike with your teeth and begin the tricky process of writing. It's not easy but you've gotten about as good at 'handwriting' as anyone who went to school after the advent of the computer. You would worry that your writing style bugs Mike or might tip him off to your secret, but confronting people in the office about incredibly bizarre things they do is a big no-no. That would be rocking the boat and if there's one thing you've learned about your office it's that it is a boat and if there's one thing you've learned about boats it's that they should not be rocked. For someone here to report you, they'd have to find you doing something truly lupine.

You scrawl down a quick 'HAPPY BIRTHDAY' and give the card back to Mike. He looks briefly at what you've signed and makes a bit of a face, as though he doesn't like it. At first you just attribute this to Mike's naturally repellant nature but then you catch a glimpse of the front of the card and see that it reads, 'Our Condolences'

'OH GOD MIKE I THINK I MISSPELLED SOMETHING, CAN I HAVE THAT BACK?'

Mike grins, mistaking this mixup for a moment of bonding, 'Sure, pal! I'm always useless before my coffee too!' You glide right past that trap he set for you and with some artful scribbling you turn 'HAPPY BIRTHDAY!' into the much more appropriate 'HAD BAD DAY!' before giving him a nod. He grabs the card and shuts it. You briefly consider asking about whatever tragedy has befallen Tamara, but you know that each moment following Mike's departure will feel like you've been given wings. You turn away from Mike and head back toward your desk to answer some e-mails in the vain hope that when you return to the breakroom, Mike will be nothing but a memory.

Turn to page 74.

IF IT IS TAMARA'S BIRTHDAY, she'll have plenty of people telling her to be happy. If it's not Tamara's birthday and you write 'HAPPY BIRTHDAY' she'll know that you weren't paying attention to her card. You like Tamara, she's kind to you. You don't want her to feel this way about you, and there's probably no way to write 'MIKE WAS THE ONE TALKING TO ME ABOUT THIS, SO YOU GET IT, RIGHT?' without him seeing it. You decide instead to write down the very safe 'WAY TO GO TAMARA!'

You ever so gently grab the pen from Mike, smashing it between your paws. As long as you can hold the pen firmly in place, you'll be able to write something brief. There's always the concern that the way you hold a pen will be off-putting to anyone who sees, but you're confident that none of your coworkers would be so taken aback by it that they'd suss out your identity. If someone does something odd in an office environment, the customary response is to ignore it completely until you use it as gossip fodder later in the day.

You write as legibly as you can, give it a once over for misspellings, and hand it back to Mike along with the pen. As he closes the card, your eyes widen with horror as you read the words 'Our Condolences'.

This is the ultimate rarity in office greeting cards: the sad greeting card. You frantically ask Mike for details, hoping maybe you're wrong or it's ironic or something.

'HEY MIKE, I'M SORRY BUT WHAT HAPPENED TO TAMARA AGAIN? YOU KNOW HOW IT IS BEFORE YOU GET YOUR COFFEE.'

Mike lets out way too big a laugh for that joke, 'No problem pal, I get it. It's Albert. He died.'

This is terrible. Albert is Tamara's pet tortoise. She had a picture of him on her desk.

'OH MY GOD NO I LOVED ALBERT.'

And it was true. Tamara had brought Albert into the office a couple times for some reason and you had taken a liking to what would prove to be the only living thing you've never had any interest in eating. You remember Tamara holding his tiny tortoise form in her hands, his legs pointlessly flailing in the air, his eyes calmly staring straight ahead. You watched him eat a cube of watermelon and experience pure bliss. A tiny, simple thing deemed deserving of centenarian status, or so he'd thought. You remember being jealous of the incredible confidence he seemed to radiate from behind the protection of his longevity and a home he carried with him wherever he went. You'd never seen peace before you'd met Albert. And you'd never known such jealousy.

'Yeah, it's really sad, she left him alone outside for a few minutes and he got hit by a car.'

'OH MY GOD WHY WAS HE OUTSIDE?'

'Oh well you know Albert, he loved being outside. She feels *terrible* about it.'

If you could sweat, you would. You just wrote 'WAY TO GO TAMARA!' in a card for a woman who is feeling incredibly guilty over the death of her pet tortoise. You MUST get that card back. Tamara seeing it could ruin everything. But before you can say anything, you see The Boss. She's entered the breakroom briefly between meetings, like the woman of the people she is. Mike, desperate for a combination of human contact and a chance to publicly submit to authority, makes a quick exit.

'Oh, there's Sharon, I'm going to grab her signature before she heads out for lunch. Catch you later big guy!'

And just like that it's over. All of it. In mere moments, your boss will see your crushing lack of sympathy for tortoises. Tamara will see it soon after. And worst of all, you've spent enough time talking to Mike to make him think it's okay to call you 'Big Guy.' He probably thinks you're friends now. You know how Albert must have felt at the end. Word of this will spread through the office quickly and you don't want to be here when it does. You have to run. You have to go back to the woods and just hope that you can cobble together some kind of life there that you won't destroy as swiftly and profoundly as the one you had here. You feel a knot in your stomach, but you know what has to be done. You rush through the hallway and into the elevator. You don't even bother to grab your bag. You don't need it anymore. You get outside and start to run. You don't care who sees you bounding through the streets because by the time they think to stop you, you'll be well past them on your way to the forest.

Turn to page 30.

SUPPOSEDLY, THERE WAS A TIME before e-mails. In this time, the workday ended when you left the office. People were forced to return home to their families and remain hopelessly disconnected from their team of coworkers until the next day. You've only heard people mention this time in passing, and since you are much younger than most of your coworkers in human years, you mostly take their word for it. But now, e-mails are one of the most powerful forces in the business world. Every day they're sent, read, and returned. They bounce back and forth from person to person, in and out like a tide. The person you are in e-mail is far different from who you are in real life. You're a refined version of yourself, unburdened by your physical form and its many limitations. Someone unremarkable out in the real world could be a living legend in the e-mail signature game. And likewise, a slip-up over e-mail could affect your real life as well. The placement of each word, each piece of punctuation has incredible meaning.

You open up your inbox to see a shockingly manageable three e-mails. This is likely due to it being Friday. As the week nears its end, people know that if they stay absolutely still, there's an elevated chance that they'll be able to leave work a single hour early: the perfect crime. Your first message is a weekly office newsletter called 'Thursday Buzz' that you ignored yesterday. Thursday Buzz serves as a weekly reminder of things you already know and also birthdays. Thursday Buzz is a trap designed to steal time from you. You did not read Thursday Buzz yesterday. You will not read it today. You press delete. Scrolling down, you see that your next inbox item is marked 'URGENT FOR ALL EMPLOYEES' and mentally prepare yourself accordingly. It's rare that something is marked as urgent. In an office, most people focus on seeming as relaxed as possible at all times, even in times of crisis. Something being referred to as urgent means that it's either very, very urgent or it's from Mike.

Hey everyone!

I am once again reaching out to everyone at the same time because yesterday my lunch was stolen out of our communal fridge for the third time this past month. Someone took my lunch, ate it, and then placed the empty Tupperware with my name on it back in the fridge and as such I believe that these are personal, targeted thefts. My wife and I meal prep our spaghetti bolognese in advance on Sunday nights. This routine is important to us and these thefts of the food we make together have made that experience a somber one for us both. Knowing that our efforts are for nothing has taken one of our favorite traditions and instead made us often cook side-by-side in silence. I hope that these senseless thefts stop so that we can forget about this once and for all.

Mike

Wow, Mike really got personal at the end there. Despite usually provoking complete apathy or, at best, mild annoyance, Mike's story makes you feel guilty for repeatedly stealing his delicious homemade pasta. However, some days you forget to bring ham or rotisserie chickens with you to work and are forced to make do with what you find. You worry that going undernourished could cause you to lose your impeccable control over your animal instincts. If Mike's lunch is the cost of keeping the office safe, you are willing to make Mike pay it from time to time. You press delete yet again.

Your day is moving along smoothly so far. You're deleting useless e-mails left and right but when you see the last item in your inbox, you feel sick. It's from your boss. The subject line simply reads 'Action Needed' but you know what it really means is trouble. You can't possibly think of anything you've done wrong, but open the e-mail to face the music regardless.

Hello,

Last night I was looking to go over notes from yesterday's sync but found that you hadn't sent them to me. Would like to know what the disconnect was here and ideally receive notes before EOD.

– Sharon

You feel as though the sheer force of that curtly punctuated e-mail could send you flying you across the room. You are devastated. You've let The Boss down. To make things worse, you weren't even at the meeting she referenced so you have no notes to give her.

This happens from time to time with The Boss. She is an incredibly busy woman who is always giving 110% which means she sometimes messes up details. Without notes to give her, there's no way to set this right without telling the truth or taking responsibility for an error you yourself did not cause. You get precious few interactions with your boss, and even fewer e-mails between just the two of you. What you do next is crucial.

If you'd like to tell the truth and let The Boss know that this isn't your fault, turn to page 78.

If you'd like to take responsibility for your boss's mistake, turn to page 82.

YOU ARE MORE THAN HAPPY to admit your mistakes when you make them. Making mistakes is a very human thing to do and you've found that it can actually help your cause to mess up from time to time. Over time, humans begin to root against anyone who is doing too conspicuously well, it's best to languish in a sweet spot where you are still incredibly stressed out but have a good hairstyle figured out. However, this particular mess is not your fault. You were not invited to the meeting and couldn't possibly have the meeting notes so there's no point in pretending. The Boss did not get where she is by blaming her mistakes on others until eventually she was promoted to a position of unquestioned power. She got there by being a team player. You're sure that she'll be gracious in understanding the miscommunication. You draft a tasteful but honest e-mail explaining the situation.

HELLO

I AM AFRAID THAT I DO NOT HAVE THE NOTES IN QUESTION AS I NEVER RECEIVED AN INVITE TO

THAT MEETING AND THUS COULD NOT HAVE
TAKEN THEM. I AM SURE THIS IS A CLASSIC MIXUP
THAT WILL NOT TROUBLE US FURTHER.

That seems fine to you. You hit send and wait patiently for all to be restored to normal. Then it hits you, forming a pit in your stomach: it is a *terrible* idea to call your boss out over e-mail. Having the ability to stand up for yourself is valued deeply in concept but in practice it's something that most humans do once, *maybe* twice in their professional lives. But now that the e-mail has been irreparably sent out into the world, you are powerless to do anything but wait. You wait for what feels like hours, constantly refreshing your inbox in terror. Upon one refresh, your inbox appears to have a new message, but it's yet another cursed update from fucking Mike. You delete the e-mail in a blind, justified rage. How dare he even consider giving you a false alarm like that in a time like this. You block Mike's e-mail. There is nothing that man has done or will do in his entire vile life that you'll need to be clued into. You will absolutely be eating his lunch today. Just as you begin to fantasize about how furious Mike will be to find his weird lunch yet again destroyed by what only can be described as 'some sort of huge dog tongue' you see your inbox update with the real deal: an unread message from The Boss.

Just saw your e-mail and wanted to check in! You actually weren't supposed to have the meeting notes because you weren't invited to the meeting. Sorry for the mixup.

Devastating. She just rephrased the information that you just told her in a way that made it sound like it was in fact her discovery. And the way she rephrased it has made you look like a big idiot who doesn't get invited to important meetings. And for bringing it up at all, you seem like a rube, foolishly thinking her mistakes are mistakes and not simply another move in her great game of fifth-dimensional business chess. There's no dancing around the fact that this was a critical misstep for you but luckily, the business world is one of second chances. There has to be a way you can impress The Boss today; you just haven't figured out what it is yet. Suddenly, Gary appears. He's come to take advantage of your misstep.

'Oof, champ, that looked rough.'

'HOW DID YOU KNOW ABOUT THAT?'

'Oh, the Head of Sales gets cc'd on all the big meeting chains, friendo and, uh, you happen to be looking at the Head of Sales. You get your schedule all messed up again, dummy?' He laughs as though this is some sort of established inside joke the two of you have despite the fact that you both obviously know that it's a bald-faced insult. Gary is getting very close to your personal space with his victory preening.

'HAHA JUST A CLASSIC GOOF, I MUST HAVE BEEN EXHAUSTED FROM CONSUMING GENTLEMAN'S POISON DURING MY WEEKLY THIRSTY THURSDAY RITUAL.'

Gary loves alcohol, his crippling dependence on it as a conversational topic and a means of socialization is a cornerstone of his personality. You know that moving the conversation toward something he can talk extensively about without saying anything will divert his attention.

'Ooh so you're a whiskey guy, I wouldn't have called that! Always took you for more of a wine fella myself.' It's likely that Gary intends this to be yet another insult, as apparently some alcohols are more synonymous with having a male sex organ than other alcohols, but the joke is on Gary because even though you've never tried it, you think red wine seems incredibly cool. It's like blood that makes you want to dance.

'Y'know, speaking of drinks, Brett, Brent, and I were going to go out for lunch, maybe grab a couple brews. Seems like you've had a rough one today, it could help take the edge off.'

Oh no. By engaging one of Gary's few interests, you've only drawn him closer to you. You try to find a way to politely decline lunch, but he's prepared for you. This was no spur-of-the-moment invite.

'I can see you hesitating, pal, but don't. I know we haven't been best pals since you've been here, but this is just a classic case of a little friendly competish that's gotten out of hand. You know how it is in the office man, we're just a couple of big dogs buttin' heads.'

Did he just say big dogs? Does he think you're a big dog? Does he think dogs butt heads?

'And it's not like you've got anything to worry about. Unless you're not who you say you are or something, but that'd be crazy.'

Gary gives a forced exhale of a laugh. You're not sure if he knows anything or if he's just overloaded with dominant masculine energy from the unearned self-celebration that was his youth, but you have to find out. You have to go to lunch with Gary.

Turn to page 86.

IT'S IMPORTANT TO BE UNDERSTANDING when a coworker makes a mistake. You know how important it is for everyone on a team to pull their weight and that sometimes part of pulling your weight means taking the blame for a mistake you didn't make. Especially when the person who made that mistake is your boss and could fire you at any moment. In the corporate world, what goes around comes around. You're confident that even if you face consequences for this, they'll ultimately be worth it in the long run.

HELLO

I AM SO INCREDIBLY SORRY. I SOMEHOW LOST THE FILE THAT CONTAINED MY NOTES! I DO NOT KNOW HOW THIS POSSIBLY COULD HAVE HAPPENED!! I AM SO SORRY FOR LETTING THE TEAM DOWN ON THIS ONE!!

You use every exclamation point you can muster. Exclamation points are the business equivalent of rolling onto your back and exposing your pale, soft belly to your superior. The more you use, the more loudly you are yelling 'YOU WIN!' at whoever's wrath you're looking to avoid. And while behaving like this for a mistake you didn't even make isn't your proudest moment, it's smart all the same. There's a reason that all the animals that can survive disasters are pathetic.

You try to think of any possible way to save face here, you still need some sort of excuse that will keep The Boss from doubting your commitment. In your early days at the company as an intern, you remember frequently having things blamed on you that were no real fault of your own. You think of Belinda, the intern assigned to your department. She very rarely messes up, so you can't imagine it would be THAT big of a deal if you tossed this on her plate. Sure, you hated it when you were an intern, but now you're not an intern, so clearly the situation has changed. This is necessary.

I THINK MAYBE I WAS SUPPOSED TO GET THE NOTES FROM BELINDA!! SHE IS USUALLY VERY ON TOP OF THINGS THOUGH SO TRULY WHO IS TO SAY!

You think that should do it. You've taken the blame, maneuvered around the consequences, and sit far enough away from Belinda that you won't have to think too hard on the implications of your decision to throw her under the bus. She's young and in debt, she'll be fine.

Suddenly, Gary arrives at your desk wearing the broad, inoffensive smile of someone who has an agenda.

'I've gotta admit, buddy, I'm impressed. You handled that like a pro.'

'HOW DID YOU KNOW ABOUT THAT?'

'Oh, the Head of Sales gets cc'd on all the big meeting chains, friendo and, uh, you happen to be looking at the Head of Sales.'

'OH TOTALLY, THAT MAKES A LOT OF SENSE, I DEFI-
NITELY KNOW WHAT THAT E-MAIL WAS ABOUT AND I
KNOW EVEN MORE ABOUT WHAT PURPOSE WE AS A
COMPANY ULTIMATELY SERVE. I THOUGHT THAT E-MAIL
WAS A SLAM DUNK.'

'Ooh, I did not see you as a b-ball man, my man! No offense,
you're just not much in the height department.' He says this with a
laugh because being six feet and two inches tall is a massive part of
Gary's personality. This slightly above average height is likely the
wellspring of his confidence, and while Gary knows nothing of the
violence you're capable of on four legs, he finds your height on two
to be laughable.

'Y'know, speaking of sports, Brett, Brent, and I were going to go
out for lunch, maybe grab a couple brews, catch highlights from the
game last night. Plus, it seems like you've earned yourself an early
one.'

Oh no, by engaging one of Gary's few interests, you've only
drawn him closer to you. You try to find a way to politely decline
lunch, but he's prepared for you. This was no spur-of-the-moment
invite.

'I can see you hesitating pal, but don't. I know we haven't been
best pals since you've been here, but this is just a classic case of a little
friendly competish that's gotten out of hand. You know how it is in
the office man, we're just a couple of big ol' alpha dogs buttin' heads.'

Did he just say big dogs? Does he think you're a big dog? Does
he think dogs butt heads?

'And it's not like you've got anything to worry about. Unless
you're not who you say you are or something, but that'd be crazy.'

Gary gives a forced exhale of a laugh. You're not sure if he knows anything or if he's just overloaded with dominant masculine energy from the parade of unearned congratulations that was his youth, but you have to find out. There's no way around this. You have to go to lunch with Gary.

———

Turn to page 86.

DESPITE YOUR BEST EFFORTS, you find yourself in the office parking garage with Gary and his two sales department subordinates, Brett and Brent. These two men are so alike in their incredible subservience to Gary that you genuinely thought that they were the same person until just now when you saw them together. While getting lunch with someone who is actively suspicious of your entire identity and his two friends who you thought were just one friend doesn't seem like an ideal situation, spending obligatory time with people you find repugnant is one of the pillars of the corporate lifestyle so you're determined to make the best of it. Gary's not particularly good company but his tireless adherence to a very traditional brand of masculinity means that his favorite restaurants are almost entirely meat-centric which works out great for you. Human men love to discuss meat. They will talk about its preparation, how good it feels to eat too much of it, or how dumb their doctors and spouses are for begging them to eat less of it. If human masculinity boiled down to meat enthusiasm, you'd have it all figured out by now, but unfortunately it involves a myriad of other, less obvious, conversational minefields.

The four of you get into Gary's spacious automobile. In a city like yours, Gary's car makes very little sense. It doesn't make effective use of fuel, it's difficult to park, and it is nice enough to occasionally get broken into without being nice enough to impress any of the people he hopes it will impress. You focus on resisting the incredible urge to stick your whole head out the window on the drive, even if you know for a fact that it would feel like you'd always imagined flying would feel. Instead you listen to Gary tell you things about his car. It has great highway mileage. It has heated seats. Periodically, Brett or Brent will say something like 'Nice!' or 'Dude, *hell* yeah' so that Gary feels affirmed but you know that your reaction to these facts doesn't matter as much as it matters that you allow Gary to say them. One thing he says does pique your interest though.

'. . . and with a trunk this big I could drive out to the forest on the weekends and camp, no problemo.'

This is just is a worst case scenario you're considering, but if Gary *is* onto your secret and you can somehow get him out to the woods for a night of pretending he's interesting by sleeping outside, you may be able to put a stop to the problem before it starts. You haven't spoken to your brother since you left the forest, but you're certain that nothing would help rebuild that relationship quite like a fresh meal. But you hope to not have to do that. You've gone this far without having to eat or murder anyone and you'd prefer to keep that streak alive. But just in case, you casually ask Gary, 'OH, HAVE YOU EVER ACTUALLY GONE CAMPING BEFORE?'

'Oh, quit busting my balls man, I've got all the gear, I'll get out there one of these days,' Gary replies with a laugh. Unfortunately,

Gary's interest in the outdoors, like most men's, mainly involves buying things he doesn't use. And now your line of questioning has metaphorically ruined his testicles. Now he's sure to try and ruin yours in response. Before you're subjected to any more car-based testicle discussion, Gary pulls into the parking lot of WING TOWN, a chicken-wing-centric eatery. He parks the car and your man-group heads for the entrance.

'Boys,' he says, 'welcome to heaven.'

You are fairly certain he would not have said that if he was just with Brett and Brent.

You walk through the doors of WING TOWN and suddenly you've left the outside world behind. The lighting is dim, presumably so that you can shamelessly enjoy beers at 11:30 in the morning. The restaurant is a temple to the concepts of meat and yelling. Each wall is lined with televisions showing any and all possible sports games, even the ones that don't really matter to anyone aside from their value as a centerpiece for drinking. Each table has a small plastic basket of popcorn, a complimentary gesture of trash food from the restaurant. You are not sure what value humans see in hot corn, but it is EVERYWHERE. A young waitress approaches your group and, horrifyingly, seems to know Gary by name.

'There he is! I thought we weren't going to see you this week!'

The waitress is young, with the clear skin of someone who still has hope for the world. At first glance, you would think that she likes Gary and is excited to see him, but the more you look at her face the more you recognize the deep disdain that most restaurant employees carry for men like Gary. Gary has never been asked to clean up someone's mess. Gary makes the mess. Gary makes the mess and somehow gets paid $75,000 a year. And for this he has earned a hatred that burns just beneath the surface of Grace's manager-mandated smile.

'You know me, Grace, I can't stay away from this place!' Gary laughs, taking his frequent patronage at a chain restaurant and mistaking it for friendship.

'I just thought you'd wait until after five!' Every moment Grace spends talking to Gary seems to push her closer to an edge and what is on the other side is known only to her.

'I like to think of Friday as one big long five o'clock.' Gary bursts out laughing at his own joke, a reference to his incredible reliance on alcohol as one of his only discernible non-business personality traits. Grace feigns a laugh, knowing that Gary won't give it much scrutiny since it's being drowned out by his own. She shows the four of you to a table. Since you are a group of four men at a wing restaurant during a workday, she seats you at a tall bar table with stools, correctly assessing that your masculinity cannot sustain the suggested intimacy of a regular table or, God forbid, a booth. This works out perfectly for you as someone who cannot sit in chairs the right way. Grace sets down a few menus and gives you a rundown of what WING TOWN offers. 'As I'm sure you guys know, we've got all our usual deals but since it's Friday, you're also welcome to try the "Escape to Wing Mountain". That's three baskets of our spiciest boneless wings and if you finish them within ten minutes, your whole table's tab is comped.'

'OH NO BONELESS?'

'What?'

'SORRY CONTINUE.'

Grace relays the rest of the specials to you. Gary orders a pitcher of beer for the table which is just as well for you. Shared alcohol is the only instance in which people want you to consume less and you've always stayed far away from the stuff. Your one encounter with coffee was a disaster and you can only assume that a brush with alcohol would be even worse. As Grace walks away, Gary makes a comment slyly to the table, 'I'd like to escape to her wing mountain.'

The comment itself makes no sense but you can tell that Gary was trying to say a sex thing about Grace. In this situation, one would think that maybe it would be a good idea to say something to Gary along the lines of 'Hey our waitress seems like she might be like twenty-one at oldest' or 'C'mon man that's not cool' but living in abject fear of the anger of men like Gary while they flourish without consequence is actually a cornerstone of the human male experience. It's best not to cause a conflict during lunch and instead vaguely hope that something is done about Gary or men like him at some point in the future.

Brett and Brent laugh, perfect servants in every way; though Brent's laugh seems strained and his eyes get a bit distant. It's as though he wonders for a moment exactly which decision brought him here to WING TOWN, where he lay prostrate to the conversational whims of a man with so little self-awareness that he thinks his waitress is interested in him romantically. Maybe he wonders if child-Brent would approve of the sacrifices adult-Brent has made for a career in sales. Or wait, maybe that's Brett.

You decide it may be a good idea to change the topic of discussion to something that doesn't remind the table of Gary's existence as a sexual being. Gary made a terrible chicken-wing metaphor, so you feel confident making one of your own.

'YOU KNOW WHAT THE REAL "ESCAPE TO WING MOUNTAIN" IS? MY JOB AS A GRAPHIC DESIGNER.'

There's no response. Brett and Brent won't even make eye contact with you until they know how Gary feels and Gary doesn't seem to have understood the statement.

'BECAUSE SOMETIMES MY JOB IS DIFFICULT MUCH LIKE IT WOULD BE FOR A HUMAN MAN TO EAT THREE BASKETS OF PATHETIC BONELESS WINGS.'

You're fairly certain the Gary still isn't 100% sure what you were trying to say, but in his defense, neither are you. Small talk with coworkers is a special type of hell reserved specifically for lunch-time and you still haven't figured out its finer points. Gary waves a hand at you as he polishes off his first lunch beer.

'Ah, c'mon man I don't wanna talk about work here. I told you, this place is my spot, I come here to relax.'

You feel profoundly sad for a moment at how earnest that statement sounds, as though this may be the closest you and Gary have ever come to actually making contact.

'C'mon, let's talk about anything else, dude.'

And just like that Gary has thrown the conversational gauntlet right back into your lap. You need to act quickly, as most humans have plenty of inane topics to discuss with coworkers ready at all times. Allowing too much of a conversational lull to form runs the risk of letting your coworkers' minds wander, something you'd prefer didn't happen when you're about to try to eat like a human in front of them. When it comes down to it, you know very little about Gary. You know he works in the Sales department, that he makes enough money to buy a Kia Sportage, and that he enjoys consuming alcohol. Your instinct says that engaging Gary's interest in alcohol by mentioning something irresistible like craft beer would take the weight of contribution off you entirely, but you worry that your lack of experience with it might be easy for an expert like Gary to suss out. It may be smarter to ask about something broader like his general weekend plans.

To discuss craft beer, turn to page 93.

To ask Gary about his weekend plans, turn to page 98.

IF YOU AREN'T ALLOWED TO TALK about work, you want to make sure that your follow-up suggestion is well received and there is no greater flame than craft beer for the moth that is the heterosexual human male. To your understanding, craft beer is far superior to regular beer. While it may be the same beverage in name, some arcane process in its creation and enjoyment gives it an extra layer of respect in the eyes of beer lovers. You've never experienced this yourself obviously. Coffee, alcohol – these liquids seem to help humans acclimate to mundane surroundings but you've found a thrill in the mundane, a beauty in the inanity of daily human life. Also you basically have dog kidneys and you're not really sure how drinking a poison would work for you. The risk of death is a major part of most male hobbies. Smoking, professional football, melted cheese, and a lifelong dedication to stoicism all have an appeal rooted in oblivion, but for most the risk is minimal in the moment and instead gets incurred over time. For you, ingesting alcohol would truly be a game of life or death. But you're fairly confident that if you ask Gary about his favorite craft beers, he'll completely dominate the conversation until Grace returns to take your order.

'GARY, I HAVE NOTICED THAT YOU ENJOY BEER HAVE YOU ENJOYED ANY PARTICULAR BEERS LATELY?'

'Oh buddy, where to begin!' Gary exhales in excitement and leans forward. 'That's the one thing about this place I don't love, they're domestic only so I usually just grab the cheap stuff, but a new favorite I've been into lately is this amber. It's called Awful Porpoise, and get this, it's aged in *whiskey barrels*.'

'WHISKEY BARRELS HOLY HELL.'

From what you've pieced together, whiskey does the same thing as beer but hurts to drink and costs more. You assume that putting beer in whiskey is better, like when you're eating meat and find a really good bone. Gary continues to go on about Awful Porpoise. At this point, you don't even have to listen. He's thrilled just to be talking. He'll blissfully go on without any regard for your opinion and especially without regard for the opinions of Brett and Brent, who you have almost completely forgotten at this point. At some point Gary will pause and it will be your turn to say something like 'YEAH' or 'TOTALLY' and then, taking that single word as proof of your interest and permission to continue talking, he will continue talking.

'It has that whiskey smokiness to it but with that rich amber flavor, y'know? I've been trying to replicate it with my homebrew but obviously I don't have space for whiskey barrels in the ol' condo so I just blow cigar smoke into it while it's fermenting and personally, I think it's pretty damn close.'

Oh no, Gary brews his own beer. You wanted to talk about something that would keep Gary occupied for a bit, but this threatens to become the sole topic of lunch discussion and if Gary asks you even one question, you may well be doomed. You try to put a button on the conversation before it spins out of control.

'WELL I WILL HAVE TO TRY YOUR BEER SOMETIME.'

You are filled with an incredible anger at yourself for making an unkeepable promise that Gary is sure to follow up on but simultaneously proud of yourself for organically experiencing the deeply human moment of saying something in a moment of panic that runs completely counter to your own needs and desires.

'Well why wait, amigo, I've got some sitting outside in the Garymobile!'

This couldn't be going worse. You've gone from calmly listening as Gary droned on about nothing to staring down the barrel of a loaded gun. You have no idea what normal alcohol will do to you if you drink it, let alone Gary's nightmarish concoction. In addition to all of this, the beer has also been sitting in a hot car for an undetermined amount of time and you always imagined your first drink being a little more special than this. If you're risking your life, it should at least be to mark something important.

'OH NO I COULD NOT POSSIBLY DO THAT. WE ARE IN A BUSINESS THAT SELLS BEER'

'Nah, it'll be fine, here let me just tell Grace.' You try to stop him from bothering Grace but it's too late, Gary is already flagging her down. She quickly waves off his question with a flippant 'You're fine, hon' without an extra moment of thought, having correctly assumed that none of this will change Gary's clockwork tip of slightly less than 15%. This needs to be stopped now before he goes out to his car.

'SERIOUSLY GARY, I CANNOT, I DON'T DRINK ACTU-ALLY.'

Gary considers this for a moment but then you see something light up behind his eyes.

'Wait a second. You told me you were hungover today from thirsty Thursday . . . '

'HAHA SORRY THERE WAS NO THIRSTY THURSDAY, THAT JUST ANOTHER ONE OF MY CLASSIC LIES.' Why would you say it like that?

'Another?'

He's putting it together. He looks at you and you can see him *really* looking at you. He's finally seeing you.

'Wait a second . . . '

You were born in the cold of an unseasonably wet spring. Like your brothers and sisters, you were blind for two weeks, smelling and tasting blood long before you saw it. Most of them didn't survive childhood but you did. And you did so because you knew that the only thing that keeps you alive is knowing when to strike first. You step back for a moment as a frantic energy you've desperately hidden for so long courses back into your bloodstream.

You lunge at Gary in a powerful display of animal engineering. Your jaw closes on his neck and you tear his throat open, causing an arterial spray that douses a shocked Brett and Brent. Their physical forms may survive today but the Brett and Brent that leave WING TOWN will be new men altogether. Your blood-soaked face will haunt their dreams.

You need to leave this place before instinct takes over completely. This lunch was a mistake, but you can still get out of this with your life. Time seems to stand still as you look at the other restaurant patrons, who stand in a stunned silence staring at Gary's limp form on the floor next to his barstool. In a booth, he could have died with some dignity. You sniff through Gary's pocket, detecting the sickly sweet scent of paper money in Gary's clip. You toss it onto the table, blood dripping from your chin. If anyone deserves to come out of today on top, it's Grace. You dart for the door and no one dares to stop you. Your claws click on asphalt faster and faster as you put WING TOWN, Gary, and the life that just this morning seemed so secure, behind you and run. There's only one place left that'll have you.

Turn to page 30.

THERE'S ABSOLUTELY NO REASON to talk about craft beer unless you have no other option. A more general inquiry into Gary's weekend plans will do just fine. He will probably be competing in a recreational sports league, meeting up with two to three other men for approximately eight beers, or enjoying a new streaming television series.

'ANY BIG PLANS FOR THE UPCOMING WEEKEND?'

Shockingly, Brent starts to answer. While Brent is essentially the same as Brett in your eyes, you're beginning to see that he's more complicated than he lets on. Maybe his association with Gary is just for professional survival. For most people, work friends are a necessity. Workplaces put their employees in the middle of complicated power dynamics with an ever-changing cast of characters, making their day-to-day lives so needlessly complex that the only people that could ever understand what they talk about at the end of the day are their coworkers. This essentially guarantees that anyone who doesn't choose to partake in their office's social structure will be unable to discuss work with anyone else, and therefore can never truly be known by anyone. But for some people that's okay. For them, jobs aren't life defining and they live rich fulfilling lives outside of them. Perhaps Brent is one of these people.

'Well actually my improv team has a show at Corn Tub, this theater over by—'

Oh God you are not getting duped into another improv show, the natural world is missing out on absolutely nothing by not having improv comedy.

'OH BOOOOOO GARY SPECIFICALLY WHAT ARE YOU DOING.'

Brent starts to scroll through his phone nervously as the conversational reins are passed off to someone who won't try to make you go to a theater that's a corn processing plant during the day.

'Oh, I'm actually hanging out with this girl I met online, we were gonna hit a wine bar tomorrow night. And that's not the only thing I'm hoping to hit if you know what I mean . . . '

Gary is being gross again but in his defense, this is likely because people like him seem to reproduce at three to five times the rate of anyone with empathy. Usually you would glide right past this, but you've actually scheduled your first human date for this very evening. You've been nervous about doing this for awhile, but it's been months since you've lost control of yourself. You feel you've proven your ability to make the next move toward your happiness. You entered this world ostensibly to feel less lonely and you believe you're finally ready to take the steps to get to that point. While you never hope to have a presence at all resembling Gary's, his insight into the notoriously awkward ritual of the first date may be useful to you.

'I ALSO DO ONLINE DATING, HOW FUN. HOW DO YOU PLAN TO BREAK THE TENSION?'

'Oh man, I just don't *let* the tension happen, y'know? I just start talking about stuff I like to do, and girls usually love that.'

If the experience of these young women is anything similar to the one you've had over the last hour or so, you have some serious doubts about whether girls really do love that. However, it's impossible to know for sure. Human society is a beautiful tapestry of different types of dumb people who are insanely horny for each other.

'The wine bar is super classy, and I always pick up the tab. You've *got* to flex that cash, man. Though I guess maybe at your salary maybe that's tough. I kid, though.'

Gary laughs at you, having just said a mean thing which is fine because he also said he was kidding, which means that the mean thing he said was cancelled out and thus any negative feelings you have about it are actually your fault. Unfortunately, it still stings. You think your salary is great. You use it to buy ham. But you may not be able to afford picking up an entire dinner and the idea that this could doom your very first date before it even starts makes you sad. You'd hope that someone would be on the date because they're excited to get to know you, not because they need help paying for twenty-eight dollars' worth of Italian food. You're not sure you like how it sounds when Gary explains dating to you.

'Plus, she's like twenty-four so she'll just be stoked to be at a wine bar. I hope she's chill, not like this last girl I was with, she went like nuts just because I wasn't like *always* available or whatever.'

Apparently, Gary is one of the many human men who finds it incredibly impressive to be unable to date partners his own age. He also seems unable to fully articulate why any of his past partners left him. Wolves mate for life, this is something you don't think you can change in yourself. When you look for a partner, you're looking for someone who knows you. But Gary seems unsure what he's looking for. You feel a little sad for Gary. You've only lived in human society for a short time, but you wonder if maybe you've figured out more of it than he has. Gary has all the signifiers of a human man, but his well-being hinges on a lack of self-awareness and if that were ever to go away, he'd likely be as lost as you are. The more you let Gary talk about the ins and outs of romantic relationships, the more upset you can feel yourself becoming.

You smell meat on the air, you should be enjoying yourself. You think maybe the perfect thing to get everyone on the same page would be taking part in WING TOWN's big special, 'Escape to Wing Mountain.' A little competition and delicious meat would do you all good. Plus, you happen to know that eating three baskets of pathetic boneless wings will be easy for you, no matter the size of the basket. Beating Gary may intensify your rivalry, but it also would get the table's check comped which could do wonders for your just barely surface-level work friendship. By the end of today, Gary either needs to see you as a trusted ally or a pathetic Brett and/or Brent level subordinate. His suspicion can't be allowed to continue. Grace returns to your table to take your order and you decide to go for it.

'GRACE, I DO NOT WANT TO SPEAK FOR MY PALS HERE BUT I PERSONALLY WILL BE TRYING OUT THE "ESCAPE TO WING MOUNTAIN".'

Gary takes the bait. As a man in his late thirties, he'll do anything reckless to seem fun.

'My man, I like your style, make that two. Actually, four! Brett, Brent, get ready for this boys. One of us has to win this thing.'

'Actually, I'm super sensitive to spicy—' Brent timidly tries to speak up to no avail.

'I think that'll do it for us, thanks Gracie.'

Grace visibly cringes at Gary referring to her so familiarly, perhaps using the same nickname as her close friends or a long-since-departed grandparent, but she shrugs it off, smiles, and bids you farewell. Word spreads quickly across the restaurant that your table will be taking part in the challenge. 'Escape to Wing Mountain' and its promise of free lunch is an alluring concept, but few people actually end up taking part. It's fun in the same way that talking about a large lottery pot is fun. A few people around you whisper in anticipation of what's to come. Soon, Grace returns with twelve baskets of wings. They're ready quicker than you'd like for what's supposed to be freshly made food, but whatever sauce they've slathered over the wings appears to have made their relative age unknowable. You have the distinct advantage of being conditioned to eat up to fourteen pounds of raw or rancid meat in a single sitting, so you know your stomach can handle whatever comes next. The rules of the competition are simple: Finish three full baskets of spicy boneless wings in ten minutes. You were built for this. Before Grace starts the clock, Gary gives you, Brett, and Brent a nod and says, 'See you on the other side boys,' with a solemn tone that lets you know this man has not even once actually considered his own mortality. That day will come, but today all Gary will be thinking about is how definitively you defeated him in this game of skill. You nod back at him. In lieu of a stopwatch, Grace grabs her phone and sets the timer for ten minutes.

'All right. Three . . . two . . . one . . . go.'

You waste no time sinking your face into the first basket. Without bones to add texture, this meat doesn't stand a chance against you. You fly through wing after wing, swallowing some whole. The sauce they're in is spicy but you're undeterred. You're just thinking about the meat. Sauce covers your face and mouth, but you do not care. You know that what's happening here right now may well be the most important competition of your life thus far. You are briefly thrown off by a coughing sound as Brent clutches his stomach. He cries out in pain.

'Oh God, I'm sorry guys, I can't do spicy stuff . . .' His face is a deep red with sickness, embarrassment, or likely both. He's right to feel this way. Even by human standards it's embarrassingly early for something like that to happen. Poor Brent apologizes to onlookers at nearby tables, many of whom could have been considered potential mates. Brett stops for a moment to check on him. He quickly sees that Gary has continued shoveling wings into his mouth without so much as diverting his attention, taking advantage of the confusion. Brett mutters what you'd imagine is an apology for his sickly friend, but you cannot hear it. You can only hear the blood rushing through your ears over the sound of your own jaws obliterating your food. You are focused on one thing and one thing only, and that thing is the mountain of affordable, medium-quality chicken wings in the basket ahead of you.

You polish off your first basket and see that Gary is close behind you. Brett is further behind, still suffering for his brief consideration of empathy. You look to your second basket of wings. You know you can finish them without a problem. However, you know that the more meat you eat, the more you become ruled by instinct.

Your kind have been hard-wired by thousands of years of evolution to eat as much meat as you can in a single sitting. This skill is in your DNA, but so is the meat fury that comes with it. You've never had this much in one sitting with so many people around. Against what feels right, you briefly entertain the idea of pretending to lose the contest. You shudder at what your family would think if they saw you now as you consider opting out of several pounds of free meat, but they aren't here. They could never be in your shoes if they tried. You left them behind because you wanted something differ-ent, and you don't want to lose control and put the life you've built for yourself at risk. But as you watch Gary close in on the end of his first basket, wing sauce spread across the dumb smirk that perpetu-ally adorns his face, you feel an almost impossible amount of contempt. This decision won't be easy.

If you think it's a bad idea, turn to page 105.

If you want to finish the second basket, turn to page 108.

YOU STARE AT THE SECOND and third baskets of wings. They cry out to be eaten, appealing to every sense you possess, but you have to play it safe. It's a hard truth to accept, but there will be more opportunities to eat meat. Perhaps in some alternate universe, you win this contest and nothing bad happens and you feel foolish for having worried. But if your life fell to pieces because of a chicken-eating contest with a man like Gary, you would never forgive yourself. And that risk isn't worth any amount of potential reward. You take a few performative bites of your remaining wings, pretending to slow down, and eventually you stop and push the basket away from you.

'SORRY FRIENDS, I THINK THAT IS ALL I CAN DO,' you say, feigning weakness.

Gary looks stunned. What was supposed to be a genuine battle, a test of your fortitude, has ended with a whimper. You lost before *Brett*. The only thing between you and last place was a pile of Brent's supposed allergy to 'spicy stuff.' You're ashamed, and the fact that this was a calculated decision made to protect yourself doesn't offer you any measure of peace. You came to WING TOWN a man, but you will leave feeling like something far less. This doesn't feel right, but then the safest choice rarely does. Shortly after you stop, so does Brett, as though the failure of two of his colleagues has given him permission to stop actively causing himself discomfort. Gary finishes his second basket of wings quietly and then looks to the third. A considerable awkwardness sets in. While you weren't the first to quit, you were the person who recommended this whole endeavor in the first place and it was generally understood that you were confident in your ability to do better than you did. Now that you've quit a third of the way into the contest, it looks like you wanted to eat a slightly above average number of boneless wings and conned three other people into a big elaborate contest just so you wouldn't feel gluttonous in comparison. And worse yet, Gary is eating alone, locked in competition with no one but himself and the growing silence at your table. Not a word is uttered as Gary works his way through his final basket of wings, one by one. He occasionally stops to curse under his breath while looking at the three of you with pain in his eyes. Without the competitive aspect of the challenge, Gary is now just a man showing off a talent that no one is particularly sure he should be proud of. He finishes his last wing to a smattering of quiet applause from those around you. This was supposed to be fun, you think to yourself, but the scene you instigated today was incredibly dark. You've made Gary feel like a fool, and whatever comes next has been wholly earned. Instead of neutralizing the feud between you, you may have given it new life. Or perhaps Gary will see this defeat as a reason to leave you alone. But as the four of you ride back toward the office in a silence that's only occasionally broken by Gary muttering something to himself like, '. . . so fucked up' or 'one goddamn basket, c'mon', it doesn't seem likely.

Turn to page 121.

GARY REPRESENTS EVERYTHING you dislike about humanity. He exudes confidence while possessing very few actual skills. He's a coward who acts like a hero. He's the type of guy who would do the middle finger in a group photo, rendering it unusable for the social media profiles of the other people in the photo. He's a man who thinks he understands how to eat a whole lot of chicken at once, but he does not understand that. You do. He's sauntered into a competition that you were born and bred to win, a competition you are prepared for in a way he couldn't possibly conceive of even if he wanted to. You want to know what it feels like to defeat this man. You tear through your second basket of wings like it's nothing. You feel the meat already giving you strength. The sauce, spicy as it may be, is no match for your body's hard-wired desire to enjoy the taste of flesh. There is no single outside force that could stop you from winning and basking in the glory of Gary's destruction. You notice in the fury of your second basket that Brett has also given up. With Brent having thoroughly embarrassed himself, Brett was all clear to bow out with minimal shame. Just as well. Those two might as well not be here. This moment is all about you and Gary. This man will learn humility. This man will learn shame. He will hopefully also see you tip 22% on the bill and feel guilty for what you can only imagine has been a lifetime of miserable gratuity offerings. He'll live in regret of the day he decided to start this rivalry with you.

But as you finish your second basket, you wonder if maybe there isn't a better victory to be had here. Gary is a nightmare of a man and embarrassing him in front of a group of strangers would feel profoundly rewarding but your goal today was to discover how much of a threat he is to your survival, not to destroy him. And if you're suspicious about someone being a secret wolf, seeing them absolutely wreck a meat-based eating competition won't necessarily assuage those suspicions. When all this is over you have to go back to an office and work with this man. The type of destruction you're daydreaming about can't just be moved on from like some sort of Facebook argument. If you beat him, you'll have to deal with the ramifications of that decision until the end of your career or Gary's – whichever comes first. And on top of all this, you worry that perhaps the excessive meat you've consumed is having an effect on your usually level-headed demeanor. You feel your heart pumping and blood rushing through your body. You want to *move*. That restlessness is great news in a forest full of things to eviscerate but maybe not great news in a chicken-wing restaurant full of people trying to enjoy a reasonably priced lunch.

The idea of letting Gary win still seems insane to you, but men like Gary tend to find a way to spin even losses into victories. You may win the contest only to find out that Gary has used his man-confidence to change the definition of victory itself. You still have time to give up just a few wings shy of the end and let him finish the contest. Or you could commit to your own victory and finish what you came here to do, letting Gary's suspicions fall where they may.

———

To beat Gary, turn to page 111.

To begrudgingly give Gary a sense of superiority, turn to page 117.

YOUR TIME IN THIS WORLD has been brief, but you've already met plenty of men like Gary. Garys always win. This isn't because they are better, but because they are told from a young age that victory is their birthright. They expect it because it's given to them and it's given to them because they expect it. A Gary swims in the type of confidence that one could only receive from being very popular in high school, having wealthy parents, or being a man of slightly above average height. That confidence allows Garys to bulldoze their way into every corner of society. Gary is one of the few reliable constants in the human world. There's a Gary in every office, in every city, in every industry. But your only concern is your Gary and today, he's going to lose. With Brett and Brent out of the picture, a few nearby tables have turned their attention to you for the main event. To his credit, Gary is right behind you. He finishes his second basket of wings just as you start into your third. You take your time, just to keep things fair and to avoid getting too much sauce on yourself. You do a pretty decent job of keeping people from suspecting you're a wolf, but being slathered in wing sauce might make that a little more difficult.

You feel *good*. You haven't had this much meat in one sitting in a long time and being back in this headspace feels right. You take a moment to glance toward Gary who's started moving steadily through his third basket. He's a disgusting sauce mess. His entire face below the eyes is smeared with a dark brown glaze and the napkin he'd tucked into his shirt is of no use anymore. You wait another moment, hoping to catch his eye. He feels your stare and looks up briefly and in his eyes you see nothing but fear. There's an incredible power in showing someone exactly who you are, even if they don't know what to call you yet. You return your attention to your wings, crossing the finish line by eating the last few in one incredible chomp. You look down at the empty basket in silence for a few moments until Grace looks up from her phone and feigns excitement, performatively clapping for you. You've done it. Several members of the staff who'd been watching from afar approach you and suddenly there's a blinding flash as one of them takes an instant photo. The brief loss of vision terrifies you and your first thought is to strike, but you manage to hold it together. You are safe, you tell yourself, you are at WING TOWN with three guys from work you sort of know. Everything is going to be okay. In fact, everything is incredible. Sure, the amount of meat you've eaten is making you want to sprint as fast as you can through the parking lot, howling at the top of your lungs but that's fairly standard behavior for human men winning this type of contest so you try not to worry. Everyone's focus is on you, but yours is all on Gary. You watch him pathetically drag a wet napkin across his face with a thousand-yard stare. You know that right now Gary is mentally weighing how best to spin this to avoid embarrassment. Perhaps he'll lash out at you

112

and say that the contest was flawed in some way. He could also decide that this sudden display of meat dominance is just further cause for suspicion about your identity. He stands up and approaches you. Everyone around you has sussed out from your deranged wing-eating that there's more to this dynamic than meets the eye and they eagerly await Gary's response to his loss. Shockingly, he puts his hand on your shoulder. You are filled with a sudden desire to tear his hand to shreds and remind him that there is no end to what he's started with you, but you manage to calm yourself down again.

'Impressive stuff my man.'

You're shocked. Gary seems to have accepted you as the alpha male, which incidentally is not actually a thing for wolves, it's just a dumb thing humans made up and blamed on wolves but you understand how important the designation is for Gary and accept the title. You're thrilled that you didn't decide to quit. That would've left you with a social stature similar to that of Brett or Brent, and the very idea of having either of their lives makes you furious. Gary finds Grace amongst your well-wishers and confirms that your completion of the challenge has secured your table a free lunch.

'And yes, drinks included but not tip,' she adds with exhaustion.

'No tip, got it! Can we get two tequila shots over here for me and the big winner? My man needs to celebrate!'

Usually, the idea of consuming alcohol would concern you, but the amount of meat you've consumed has given you an incredible adrenaline rush that's made you positive that you can do anything. Sure, your kidneys weren't meant to process alcohol. But you weren't meant to bathe in the glorious warmth of human masculinity and yet here you are. Today is a big day for firsts. God, you feel incredible. When Grace returns with the shots, you figure that rather than trying to delicately lift it to your mouth like you usually would, you can lap yours up out of the glass off the tray. Who cares how you drink things? You're a contest winner.

As it turns out, everyone cares. In fact, this immediately seems to have been a bad idea because a man screams at your obvious wolf tongue. You turn to see that the screaming man is Brent. You feel a sudden warmth around your ears and a power in your bones. Brent seems very upset at the way you're looking at him and other people are taking notice; it's ruining the good vibes. You lunge toward him.

———

Turn to page 115.

YOUR HEAD IS THROBBING. Your head is throbbing and you're on the ground. Your head is throbbing and you're on the ground and you're only wearing a tie. You stand up quickly and your head hurts even more. You have to find your work clothes or someone will see you. You open your eyes and try to let things come into focus, but you smelled the blood before you'd even opened them. You're still at WING TOWN but it's quiet. You don't see a single other person in there. Windows are broken, the front doors are flung open, and sports games on the television play to no one. You're surrounded by and covered in unidentifiable blood and viscera. You close your eyes again briefly for a moment's relief, taking a deep breath. Maybe it's not as bad as it seems. You find the table you'd been sitting at with Gary, Brett, and Brent and confirm that things are exactly as bad as they seem. You absolutely killed Brent, that much is apparent right away. He's lying right where you last remember him, short of one leg. That is *classic* you – you always go for the femoral artery when you're in a good mood. You don't see Brett, but you assume that his and Brent's symbiotic relationship wouldn't allow for him to survive long without his counterpart. The only missing piece seems to be Gary until you look down and realize that the blood-soaked tie you're wearing is not your own. It's Gary's. You look for Gary's body, but you can only seem to smell it. Without any identifiable Gary bits to follow, you start to assume that maybe the wing contest left you hungrier than you'd thought, as you've always had a thing for consuming your enemies. Mixing meat fury and alcohol may not have been a great idea. You hear sirens approaching and it occurs to you that you may not be able to go back to work today. You see a full squad of police vehicles pull up outside the restaurant. They've even brought their tank. Every police department has a tank that they don't need but are incredibly and horrifyingly excited to use.

Part of you always thought it would end like this. One final battle, evenly matched in a fight to the death. You sprint outside to face your foes. The officers all begin yelling and draw their weapons as the tank advances upon you. You close your eyes and surge forward. Whatever comes next will be destiny.

————

Wow, that could not possibly have gone worse! You ruined lunch and an otherwise successful chain restaurant and also ate some of your colleagues. Your story is over.

VICTORY ON GARY'S TERMS isn't victory at all. Sure, you could eat more chicken wings than him, but then he'd just decide that chicken is stupid, or contests are dumb, or that you're dumb for even caring about winning to begin with. You cannot win against Gary unless you decide to play a different game. You're going to get dangerously close to winning the contest. Then, just as the promise of victory overwhelms him, you're going to bow out. He'll likely gloat but you're playing the long game. After today, Gary will think you're just another Brett or Brent. The thought of that makes you upset but you know that the only truth that matters is your own. You're not Brett or Brent. You're a goddamn wolf. And you'll live to fight another day. You watch as Gary closes in on his last few wings and you let him catch up with you, little by little. You give up just enough momentum to bring the two of you into a head-to-head for the final bites. You stay neck and neck with Gary until you see him take hold of his last wing. As you watch him bite in, you take the slightest pause. Mere moments pass, and Gary takes the lead just in time to win. What may have looked like simple discomfort or hesitation to any onlookers was actually you pulling off the most masterful business power-move of your career. Gary throws his slimy, sauce-covered fists in the air as he realizes his victory. The man looks like a complete wreck, covered in his own food waste. He thinks he won today. As though proving that he could eat a lot of chicken would make you feel bested on some level that would affect your workplace confidence. Though maybe winning is just a matter of being convinced that you didn't lose. Sure, Gary is covered in sauce on a Friday afternoon in a chain restaurant he frequents while surrounded by coworkers that either fear or despise him. But he has a smile plastered across his face as though he's just been given the most incredible news of his life. Gary will probably never know how ridiculous he is, but you will. And you'll wonder how with all your self-awareness, you still manage to find yourself vying for the respect of a man who unironically calls his Kia Sportage the Garymobile. And what's more human than being trapped in the shadow of a man like that?

In winning the contest, Gary secures a free lunch for you all, and at least on that level you're grateful. After he's done accepting his congratulations from strangers, he returns to you, Brett, and Brent. The man is somehow walking with more confidence, though you're unsure if this is because of his victory or because of the free alcohol he's been drinking.

'Well, fellas, you put up a good fight out there. You can thank me later for the free grub.'

You know you won't be killing Gary today, but the urge to do so washes over you as you hear him say the word 'grub'. Brett and Brent bestow their professionally mandated congratulations in the form of as many 'Hell yeahs' and 'Dude, SO dopes' as they can muster. You leave, absolutely certain that Gary didn't tip Grace after that spectacle. On the car ride home, Brett and Brent sit quietly on their phones, and Gary takes the chance to level with you, man to man.

'Y'know what dude?' he says with the slur of someone who just slammed three drinks at lunch, 'You're a good guy. Honestly I was kinda freaked out by you for awhile. You came outta nowhere and that made me nervous, but you're a fun dude. This was a good time; we should do it more often.' And just like that, Gary's thrown off your trail. You take a moment to be proud of yourself. Not only did you make the responsible (though regrettably meat-light) choice to throw the contest, but you hit a major human milestone along the way. You finally have a work friend. This is a relationship any human can hold close and cherish until the exact moment that person betrays them for personal gain, usually within that fiscal quarter. But the moments leading up to that are going to be beautiful. As the Kia Sportage nears the office, you realize that you've just made your life a little easier while also getting to eat four pounds of meat. Maybe sometimes you *can* have it all.

Turn to page 121.

AS YOU RE-ENTER THE OFFICE your clothes smell slightly of sauce, but you know that conspicuous signs of an off-campus lunch are simply just another way to signal to your coworkers that you're a normal human man. After all, it's Friday. The weekend is nearly upon you. Weekends are the only days that humans have to pursue their own ends. While two out of seven days for the pursuit of one's self-actualization may seem fairly light, you try to be grateful for what you have, even if it seems structurally flawed. After all, nature doesn't offer any days off. It's incredibly exhausting to wake up every day and know that you're going to have to battle against forces outside of your control, relying mostly on luck and hoping blindly that the outcome will be in your favor. The idea of doing that every day for a decade or so before something decides to eat you is incredibly depressing. As a part of human society, you now only need to worry about that for five out of every seven days over a much, much longer period of time. Sure, you have to work hard to make money just so you can do things that used to be free for you, like sleeping outside or eating raw chicken, but the existence of weekday drudgery has made weekend relaxation that much sweeter. To understand the weekend is to understand humanity itself. And in understanding that, you've discovered that Fridays are an incredibly important day for humans. While they share the same general structure as any other workday, their proximity to the weekend means that work is completely optional. Simply existing so close to the weekend causes humans such incredible and anxious euphoria that they can't possibly be troubled to get anything done. The day is spent idly wasting time until the first possible minute you can find an acceptable reason to escape. You wonder sometimes why you have to come to work at all on a day that seems designed to undermine it, but you assume that if Friday became the weekend, Thursday would become the new Friday, and the cycle would continue until society itself collapsed into chaos. This sort of high-volume stuff is what you've always assumed bosses get paid so much money to think about. They are the last line of defense between society and the weekend. Their harsh guidance protects the world from drowning in too much of a good thing. It's their dark purpose to listen when their employees say, 'Hey I finished up early for the day, I'm gonna hit the road,' and to look them in the eye and say, 'Actually can you check your inbox real quick?' For such a horrid burden, six figures seems hardly enough. But you try not to get too sad dwelling on how hard the executive lifestyle seems. You need to figure out what you're planning on doing with the rest of your day. Your original plan for the evening had been to go on your very first human date. After months of finessing your online dating profile into something that wouldn't immediately out you as a wolf, you believe you've smoothed out your personality enough to seem a perfectly adequate match for a human woman.

After a bit of brief back and forth messaging with a woman named Brittany Ranes, who apparently goes by 'Britt', the two of you have decided to meet for dinner tonight at a nearby Italian restaurant. Despite having messaged each other, you really know nothing about Britt other than the fact that she's a dog lover and, based on one of her profile photos, she has been to a mountain. Though when it comes to human dating, it would seem that knowing that someone likes dogs is like knowing less than nothing about them. But you hope your distant relationship to mankind's favorite coward makes breaking the ice a little easier. At any rate, you're excited to learn more about her and human courtship in general. But, there's also that retirement party for Hank that your boss reminded you about this morning. You haven't interacted with Hank much in your time at the company, but you know that humans revere their elders just as wolves do. Hank's dedication to the company is something you could learn from. Hank is experiencing a substantial milestone and you'd love to see how the office celebrates it while also trying to figure out what Hank has done to integrate so seamlessly into the workplace that he is still there well into his elderly years. You also know that a corporate executive who's in town for a number of high-level meetings will be in attendance: you could meet your boss's boss. This man is likely a font of business knowledge that you should be eager to soak up during your free time.

You're torn between your choices. Missing the date would mean abandoning poor Britt without notice, a habit known as ghosting that consists of getting to know a person just enough to damage their self-esteem to its core with your silence, making them question if dying alone in a cabin would really be so bad. It's fairly common. But missing Hank's retirement party would mean passing up on an opportunity to show your workplace how grateful you are by giving it more of your time for no extra pay. You'd hate to inadvertently disrespect Hank by not using his advanced age as an excuse to network for personal gain. But balancing your work life with your personal life is one of the greatest human challenges there is and you're excited to throw yourself at it with everything you have. It's time to make the choice that all humans must make at one time or another. What matters more to you? Your work life or your personal one?

If you want to go on your date as planned, turn to page 125.

If you want to ghost your date to attend a stranger's retirement party, turn to page 147.

HANK HAS EARNED EVERY OUNCE of his retirement party. You're sad to have to miss it but ultimately every human has to make a choice at some point about what type of person they are. Some people are willing to throw their personal lives aside to invest themselves in their careers, believing that a successful career can push everything else into place. Until recently you thought you were one of those people. You've always called your coworkers things like 'teammates' and 'family' but if you're honest with yourself, you've felt just as isolated amongst them as you did in the woods. While your shared experience means you'll always have something to talk to coworkers about, eventually the words start to feel hollow and you start to think that you'd prefer not to talk to these people at all. You've found yourself thinking more about the woods lately and you're unsure why. Even after everything you've had to go through to integrate yourself into society, you're still glad that you left your old life behind. You didn't hate the way things were, but it never felt right. Feeling so out of place while surrounded by those that belonged without trying was exhausting, and before too long you found yourself feeling like a fraud. When you left, you knew nothing about where you were going other than the fact that it was different, and in knowing that that was enough, you knew you'd made the right choice. Or at least that's what you've always told yourself. But you've found yourself feeling lonely again and that's scared you, because if running away from your life didn't make things better, you aren't sure what would. So, you've resolved to go all in on your humanity. You've been isolating yourself to survive but it's time to stop living around the humans and start living with them. It's time to date.

You cut out of the office at half past four, something you never would've allowed yourself to do yesterday. But making changes means taking some risks. Britt had done you what she thought was a favor by saying that you could pick the restaurant for dinner, but regrettably your knowledge of local eateries extends only to those that sell affordable rotisserie chickens. None of those places seem to have the ambiance necessary for a date. You're pretty sure that human dates require dim lighting and slightly fancier than normal attire to create confusion and add pressure to meeting a complete stranger with whom you may spend the rest of your life. Luckily, plugging the words 'GOOD MEAT FOOD DATE' into a search engine directed you to an Italian restaurant right by the office, Il Fratello Bagnato. Italian food is incredibly wolf-friendly. Italians in general are incredibly wolf-friendly, apparently even going so far as to let a wolf breastfeed the two founders of their capital city. That seems like a weird first interaction between wolf and man but you're not one to judge. You had originally questioned if it was a good idea to center such a sensitive event around a full meal, but it makes sense when it dawns on you that, even if this first date is a total bust, you'll get to try a totally new meat-based cuisine tonight. Even if the date goes terribly, you can still eat a bunch of lamb.

You arrive outside at the restaurant and get situated at a table. You're first to arrive so you have a moment to collect your thoughts before your date arrives. This is a big step for you. For as long as you've been a part of human society, you've been on your own. The day-to-day stress of surviving in this world has kept you distracted but you've gotten by on the hope that someday you'd meet someone that you'd enjoy spending your time with. When you made your dating profile, you didn't expect any matches. Your photo wasn't ideal and the only information you'd listed about yourself was 'COFFEE LOVER, GRAPHIC DESIGNER, DEFINITELY NOT A WOLF PRETENDING TO BE A MAN' which you think gets all your points across pretty succinctly but also doesn't really represent who *you* are. Truthfully, it was just an amalgam of things you saw on other dating profiles paired with a gentle reminder that you are a human man. You don't even know what graphic design is, really. It's something to do with fonts?

As you wait on Britt, who says she will be wearing a striped dress, you start to feel nervous. What will you even talk about? You know all the things that humans *should* talk about on dates (hiking, study abroad trips they went on almost a decade ago, and the concept of dogs) but those aren't things you're actually interested in. You're interested in ham, running really fast, and trying to understand the human world. You wonder if maybe this is a chance to let someone know more about you. You don't necessarily have to share all your secrets at once – even in the woods oversharing was generally considered a red flag – but if you're going to spend your time with someone, you at least want them to have a somewhat clear picture of who you actually are. But maybe the fate of all humans is to never be known. Maybe being human means feeling internally complex but also feeling completely incapable of communicating that complexity to anyone. Then, whenever someone asks what you like to do, you just panic and say 'Read' even though that's one of the very first things they teach every human to do. You suddenly spot a flourish of striped cloth by the door. Britt's here. Who are you going to be tonight?

If you plan to say exactly what you think a human should say, turn to page 129.

If you want to let your true self shine, even if it means taking a risk, turn to page 141.

RELATIONSHIPS ARE LONG, especially considering that wolves mate for life. If you and Britt make it through the courtship process, you'll have time to tell her how much you love ham. Romantic relationships are all about sneaking your personality into someone's life in relative secrecy, like a Trojan horse. A Trojan horse is some human story about how all the best parts of a horse are hidden on the inside of the horse. In the meantime, you have to demonstrate your viability as a mate in the traditional human fashion.

Britt makes her way to the table and sits down across from you. From everything you've learned about dating, first impressions are incredibly important. You need to make sure you lead with the self-assured confidence of a perfectly normal human man.

'Sorry I'm late! My rideshare took forever and I typically try to avoid taking the bus.'

'NO PROBLEM AT ALL, I HAVE NOT BEEN THINKING ABOUT HAM. INSTEAD I HAVE BEEN THINKING ABOUT HOW MUCH I ENJOY PRESTIGE TELEVISION SHOWS.'

Incredible, couldn't have been easier. You're already off to a great start. The waiter comes and takes your orders. You order lamb with the relaxed confidence of someone who is ambivalent toward meat. You're just a normal guy eating a normal dinner. You two exchange some casual pleasantries as you learn that Britt works in an office similar to your own. She has a dog. She's curious if you like dogs. You're not a huge fan if you're being honest. Dogs have a certain uncanny valley effect on you, like a relative who can't recognize you. They're small cowards who rely on others to pee and this feels unacceptable. You don't want to lie to Britt but also you feel that saying you don't both feel the same way about everything would lead to unnecessary conflict between the two of you. There's plenty of time in the future to reconcile your differing opinions on dogs. Tonight is about getting comfortable with each other.

'I LOVE DOGS, I THINK IT'S ACTUALLY COOL THAT MANY OF THEM HAVE BEEN BRED SO POORLY THAT THEY CANNOT BREATHE RIGHT. THAT'S A GOOD IDEA AND I THINK IT'S COOL THAT PEOPLE MADE THAT CHOICE.'

'Aww but I love pugs.'

Pugs are a travesty and a crime against nature. Their very existence infuriates you.

'ME TOO PUGS ARE INCREDIBLE. THE ONLY THING I LOVE MORE THAN PUGS WAS STUDYING ABROAD IN COLLEGE.'

You're all over this. You've been hitting your talking points every chance you get, and Britt seems interested! She laughs at things you say sometimes, and she seems to like all the same things you're saying you like. You feel like you're winning her over *and* you're having fun! During the meal you get to try an entire sauce made of meat. First dates always seemed so scary to you but this one feels like it's going about as well as it could. Sure, you're essentially talking about nothing but you're enjoying each other's company because you are avoiding having to be alone with your thoughts. That's one of the biggest goals of dating. You seem poised for a perfect human relationship. The waiter returns to your table as you finish your meals and asks if you want dessert and some coffee.

'Should we go for it?' Britt asks hopefully. Humans can only enjoy dessert if someone else agrees to enjoy it with them or else their decision to order it will be seen as a display of decadence so blatant that it borders on the offensive. You don't usually eat sugary things as they offer your digestive system very little, but everything is going so well. You'd hate to mess this up at the end of the night.

To indulge in a treat, turn to page 132.

If you politely decline, turn to page 135.

YOU LET BRITT PICK THE DESSERT since you're not experienced in that department. She seems more comfortable around you now. Maybe it's just the wine but you feel like you've made a real connection tonight.

'HOW WAS YOUR FOOD? DID YOU ENJOY THE FISH?'

'Oh, it was great! I'm so full, I can't believe I'm eating more but I always have room for tiramisu. I still can't believe you've never had it!'

'HAHA YEAH I LOVE TRYING NEW THINGS.'

Every human claims to love trying new things despite having an almost visceral negative reaction to change of any kind.

'And your lamb was good?'

'IT WAS SUPER GOOD, SOMETHING ABOUT THE SHEEP BEING SMALLER MAKES THE MEAT BETTER.'

'I'm honestly not much of a red meat girl myself.'

'OH NO BUT THAT'S THE COLOR IT SHOULD BE.'

'I know, my parents were vegetarian, so I never ate much growing up, now it just makes me feel gross.'

You feel a pang of sadness. While her reasons for not eating red meat seem valid, you can't help but be disappointed that the two of you will never be able to share in a joyous feast on the bones of a freshly killed horse, deer, or even raccoon. The waiter arrives and sets down your desserts. You take a few bites of it and feel your stomach tense up a bit. It tastes how coffee smells and the texture feels slimy. Something about it isn't right. But Britt's really enjoying it and you don't want to make her feel like you aren't, so you eat as much as you can until the rumbling turns to outright pain. Your vision blurs and your pulse quickens. Is this what all coffee-flavored foods do??

'HAHA BRITT ,JUST AS A CLASSIC GOOF COULD YOU TELL ME WHAT IS IN THIS ITALIAN DESSERT SLIME.'

'Oh man, it's the perfect combo. It's these little cookies dipped in coffee and wine, slathered up in this incredible sugary cheese mixture and topped off with cocoa.'

There are like three things in that list that upset your stomach and at least one that you're pretty sure is outright poison. You need to get somewhere where you can vomit, or your entire life may be at risk.

'Are you okay? You're kind of . . . panting.'

Your tongue is absolutely out of your mouth and you're swaying back and forth a bit as you lose control of your vision. It's sad to think that your first date is ending this way, but you need to prioritize your survival right now. You attempt to stand up from your chair, steadying yourself on the table with one paw.

'SORRY BRITT TURNS OUT I AM A RUDE MAN, I'M GOING TO BE A GHOST NOW, I WISH YOU LUCK.'

You try to take a step but fall to the ground. Britt rushes to your side, as does a member of the waitstaff. They get in close to you and it's suddenly very easy for them to see exactly who you are. The waiter says it first.

'Oh my god . . . it's some sort of huge dog . . .'

———

You accidentally ate chocolate and revealed yourself! Also, everyone at the restaurant mistook you for a big dog which is incredibly humiliating for you. Even if your body recovers from this poisoning, your ego never will. Your story is over.

MANY OF THE INGREDIENTS that are central to the appeal of dessert also happen to be things that make your organs start to shut down. You don't want to embarrass Britt by making her think the idea was bad, so you come up with a quick excuse.

'I WISH I COULD ENJOY DESSERT BUT UNFORTUNATELY I AM NOT EATING PROCESSED SUGAR RIGHT NOW. IT IS PART OF A DIET.'

You've heard several of your coworkers talk about dieting and foods they can't eat. They go on and on about food sensitivities and metabolic cleanses and sugar addiction and it seems to greatly entertain them.

'Oh no way! I'm not eating bread right now!'

'NO WAY.'

'Yeah! I found out I have a gluten sensitivity, it sucks.'

'YES, IT MAKES MY LIFE LESS ENJOYABLE AS WELL AND YET MY SIZE CONTINUES TO REDUCE IN A WAY THAT IS CONSIDERED DESIRABLE.'

'But I wake up with so much energy, I think it's good for me.'

'OH YEAH BIG TIME ENERGY, IT IS ALMOST AS THOUGH MY BODY COULD NOT PROCESS SUGAR IF IT TRIED.'

'That's how I'm starting to feel with bread! But I think I'll always miss pizza.'

'OH YES, I WILL ALWAYS LOVE PIZZA.'

Pizza is as close to a shared deity as humankind has come. To disparage it in any way is to risk oblivion. Luckily, it's also good as Hell. Britt smiles.

'God, we have so much in common.'

Turn to page 137.

FIVE YEARS LATER

TRAFFIC WAS HELL. Your rideshare pulls into the cul-de-sac and drops you off. Your home looks immaculate. A big, colorful house with a beautifully trimmed lawn. You're forty-five minutes later than you'd planned so you rush inside the house. The whole family tries to eat dinner together on Wednesdays, but you see Britt finishing her plate as you walk in. She looks annoyed.

'LOOK, I'M SORRY. I KNOW I'M LATE BUT THERE WAS A BIG CALL WITH CORPORATE AND I HAD TO STICK AROUND FOR A FEW MINUTES SO I HIT THE WORST CHUNK OF RUSH HOUR.'

She shakes her head, 'It's one night out of the week. You can't take one goddamned night a week to leave a little early? Don't you give them enough of your time?'

'OH, SO THAT'S WHAT WE'RE GOING TO DO TONIGHT, WE'RE GOING TO FIGHT?'

'Brandon and I waited for as long as we could, but he was

hungry. I understand that work is intense right now, but he doesn't. If you don't leave early for me, at least do it for him.'

'YOU THINK I DON'T WANT TO HAVE DINNER WITH MY SON?'

'It doesn't matter what you *want* to do, it matters what you're doing! And right now, you're missing out on his life.'

'I DO THIS TO PROVIDE FOR US!'

'Don't yell, he'll hear us!'

'I AM ALWAYS YELLING.'

Neither of you can meet the other's eyes. You walk to the counter and pour yourself a drink and balance it between two paws like an old pro.

'I'M SORRY. IT WILL GET EASIER SOON.'

'How long have we been saying that for?'

You swish your drink around and watch the ice as it starts to melt.

'WHERE IS HE?'

'Outside.'

You open the back door and step out onto your patio and watch as Brandon fiddles with his toys in the yard. He looks peaceful. You'd always worried that he'd have to deal with what you dealt with but he's normal as can be. In fact, he's nothing like you at all. Maybe part of you wishes in some way that he had been.

You're a wolf, but no one knows. Everyone at work sees you as another fine, if somewhat odd, coworker. The neighbors see you as a friendly member of the community. Your family sees you as a perfectly average father and husband. Even you forget what you really are sometimes. When you do remember, it's late at night when you can't fall asleep. You throw the sheets off yourself and stare at the ceiling. The only thing you can think about is what it would feel like to run through the trees until you've forgotten where you are, vanishing completely.

'BRANDON, COME INSIDE,' you say, 'IT'S GETTING DARK.'

––––––––

Congratulations! You only bonded with your partner on a superficial level and now live in an impenetrable suburban malaise! This is one of the most human things you can do!

THE END.

HUMANS CYCLE THROUGH MANY RELATIONSHIPS in their lives, but wolves mate for life. It's in your nature to be in this for the long haul once you've chosen a partner. You would never want to be trapped with someone who didn't understand who you really are. You're going to try to give this woman the fullest picture you can of who you are. Britt makes her way to the table and sits down across from you. From everything you've learned about dating, first impressions are incredibly important. You need to make sure you seem approachable.

'Sorry I'm late! My rideshare took forever and I typically try to avoid taking the bus.'

'NO PROBLEM AT ALL, I HAVE JUST BEEN THINKING ABOUT HOW ITALY HAS FOUR TYPES OF HAM.'

You're doing great, that couldn't have been easier. Best of all, Britt seems interested.

'Oh wow! I didn't know that!'

'YES, THEY REALLY KNOW HOW TO DO RIGHT BY THEIR MEAT.'

'That's so cool!'

'DO YOU HAVE OTHER MEATS YOU ENJOY?'

Britt perks up, excited, but then seems to recoil a bit.

'Oh well, I dunno. I don't think about meat that much, really. Not more than normal at least.'

'OH YEAH ME NEITHER, VERY NORMAL NUMBER OF THOUGHTS ABOUT MEAT AND BLOOD FROM ME.'

'Did you say blood?'

'OH YES SORRY I SAID IT BECAUSE I THOUGHT I HEARD YOU SAY IT.'

'No, I wouldn't say that. I never think about blood. I also don't think about bones.'

You're confused how this turned so quickly. One minute you were enjoying each other's company and now she suddenly seems nervous. Maybe you leaned too deep into all the meat and blood talk. But you love meat and blood. You'd want anyone you'd potentially spend your life with to love it too.

'I AM SORRY IF I TALKED TOO MUCH ABOUT BLOOD.'

'No, no, you're okay.' There's an awkward pause. 'So do you like dogs?'

'I THINK EVERY DOG IS A COWARD THAT PALES IN COMPARISON TO EVEN THE WORST WOLF.'

Okay it might benefit you to ease up on the honesty a little bit. There's painting a complete picture and then there's blurting out everything that pops into your head. Britt seems confused.

'You'd rather have a wolf than a dog?'

'YOU CANNOT HAVE A WOLF AS SOME SORT OF PET, THEY ARE TOO POWERFUL TO BE SUBJUGATED IN THAT WAY.'

'Oh wow, you have a lot of opinions about wolves.'

'SORRY, I'M JUST NERVOUS.'

'No, it's okay. Me too.'

You start to look at Britt more closely. You realize you've been spending so much time in your head thinking about yourself and what you want to say that you haven't paid much attention to the person you're actually with. And the closer you look, the more it starts to come into focus for you. She's a goddamn wolf. You see her clear as day now.

'HOLY HELL, ARE YOU A WOLF?'

She gasps and looks around.

'Shut up! Someone is going to hear you!'

'SO YOU ARE!'

'Shut up!!'

'NO, IT'S OKAY, I AM ONE TOO.'

'Yeah, I figured that out the second you yelled at me about ham. You're not very subtle.'

You're blown away. You've never met someone else like you. You thought you were the only creature to ever pull this off.

'HOW DID THIS HAPPEN?'

'I don't know, probably the same way it happened for you? I didn't like the woods. Now I'm here.'

'DO YOU LIKE IT HERE?'

'It still confuses me, but it beats sleeping outside.'

'YEAH AND EVERYTHING IS FOOD HERE.'

'Oh, that's the best part. There's meat everywhere and if you want something fresh, there's always something small running around.'

'SOMETIMES IF I GET HUNGRY AT NIGHT I GO TO THE PARK AND EAT RACCOONS.'

'I DO THAT TOO!' Britt catches herself and quiets down a bit, looking around. 'I'm still shocked sometimes by how little people notice. Or maybe they notice and don't care?'

'OH NO THEY WOULD CARE; PEOPLE ARE TERRIFIED OF WOLVES.'

She laughs, 'That's true.'

'SORRY I STILL CAN'T BELIEVE THIS.'

'Me neither. What should we do?'

You think about that for a moment. You finally found someone who will understand your plight and who experiences it themselves. They may not be the human you'd assumed you'd end up with, but maybe this is better. Maybe together you'll have twice the chance of getting by.

'WELL IT'S AFTER DARK. IF WE WENT TO THE PARK THERE'D BE A LOT OF RACCOONS OUT.'

'You want to go eat raccoons right now?'

'YEAH WHY NOT? WE HAVEN'T GOTTEN OUR FOOD YET AND NOBODY'S PAYING ANY ATTENTION TO US. THERE ARE ALWAYS OTHER NIGHTS TO ENJOY FOUR TYPES OF HAM.'

'Okay, but that's a little wolf-y. We should do something human after to balance it out.'

'WHAT IF WE WENT TO A BANK AND USED AN ATM AFTER?'

'I'm listening . . . '

'AND THEN WE COULD WATCH A PRESTIGE TELEVISION

SHOW AND TALK ABOUT HOW WE OVERINDULGED
DURING DINNER.'

'Perfect.'

'ARE YOU READY TO GO?'

Britt nods at you and smiles. As if on command, you both leap
out of your chairs and dart out of the restaurant through a sea of
confused humans, gone in a blur. The two of you sprint toward the
park under the light of a full moon.

————

**Woah! Your date turned out to be also a wolf pretending to
be a person! Neither of you knows exactly what you're
doing but the companionship you've found in each other
will make all the confusing parts of human life a little
easier to face. Now you have someone to eat ham with.**

THE END.

AFTER EVERYTHING YOU'VE BEEN THROUGH today to secure your position at work, you'd hate to cause trouble for yourself by missing an optional work social event. You don't want to show disrespect for Hank's big achievement and you especially don't want your boss to think that you like going to places that aren't work to talk to people that aren't coworkers. Plus, the presence of The Executive could mean that this is the type of party where big business deals are made. Many people believe that the most important part of a job is the quality of your work, and often this is true, but if you can prove to an executive that you're mildly fun to hang out with, you can bypass all of that. You have a feeling in your gut that's telling you to make sure you're at that retirement party, and you've only got this far because you know when to trust your gut.

It saddens you to have to skip your very first date, as Britt seemed nice, but part of you is relieved. The difficulty you've experienced finding a genuine connection in this world has been discouraging. Most of your social interactions are transactional. The few that last longer than a few sentences seem to all happen only because someone wants something from you or is suspicious of you. Today was the first time anyone's invited you out to lunch, and all Gary wanted to do was establish dominance over you through the demonstration of various masculine behaviors. You never felt like anyone knew you in the woods, so you left the woods, but when you came here, that feeling didn't go away. The few times you ever got someone to like you have felt unearned, like you were being rewarded for being especially good at lying that day. But work at least is honest about its ruthlessness. Gary may never be your true friend, but he was never going to be. In the office, everyone's number one priority is work and all interpersonal relationships are ultimately in service of that priority, even if they don't seem like it. The vulnerability you briefly show a coworker may be what they use to destroy you later on, or perhaps you were only vulnerable in the first place to make them feel at ease before you destroyed them. Work offers simple predator and prey relationships, like a crucible of your two worlds. The impulsivity and emotionality of humankind sits alongside nature's cruelty and its immovable hierarchy of the powerful and powerless. You may not fully understand either world, but your ability to exist in both brings you some measure of pride.

The party is at a trendy and conveniently work-adjacent bar, Corb. This works out perfectly because anyone that was thinking of leaving early will get to stay at the office until the end of the day before they can make an appearance at the party, thus preventing them from being persuaded by family or non-office friends to leave the office during their free time. You spend the rest of your afternoon doing what most of your coworkers are doing: staring straight ahead in absolute silence and letting your mind wander. When your clock hits 4:50, you stand up, grab your backpack, and head to the company's lobby. Leaving early feels wrong but conversing with people in between different settings is incredibly stressful for you, as most of your energy goes into walking as normally as you can. You don't want to leave at the same time as everyone else and end up jammed into a crowded elevator or stuck making small talk for an entire two-block walk with Mike. Corb is only a ten-minute walk away but you'd never want to spend that much time talking to Mike about his and his wife's continued participation in a recreational softball league. Plus, The Boss or The Executive could see you with him and begin mentally associating the two of you. This is the sort of damage a reputation cannot recover from. You'll walk to Corb alone. But first, you'll kill a little time hiding in the single-stall 'family' bathroom that the company offers in lieu of any sort of daycare or extended maternity benefits. This bathroom is slightly larger than other bathrooms and intended for only one person at a time. It has a small fold-out table so that parents could in theory change their child's diaper. You briefly feel bad for taking over this generously provided parental oasis for a few minutes, but you've never actually seen a child at work. The gesture is more ceremonial, and the actual presence of a child would likely be both upsetting and unwanted. You wait until 5:00, and then 5:05, and then 5:10. As you hear the office noise die down, you swing the door open and exit the bathroom with your usual post-restroom declaration of 'DID A HUGE ONE IN THERE.' You know spectacularly little about human bathroom etiquette due to its private, individual nature, but you do know that it's fine for some reason when human men talk about processing large bowel movements. A few coworkers give you a brief look, but they quickly return to their Friday afternoon activities. You make your way out the door like a pro.

You enter Corb to see that the party has already begun. The restaurant's dim lighting immediately signals it as both a place of importance and a place where you can make use of your naturally impressive low-light vision. The entire restaurant looks like it was designed to look like a human's version of the woods. Nearly every surface is wooden and made to look rougher than it is. Each table is a large slab of wood. The bar is an even larger slab of wood on top of a different type of wood. The lights look dated and bad, which is how you know they are nice. The floor is covered in some sort of ornate but messed-up tile. The office seems to have rented out the whole place, even going so far as to invest in a large spread of high-class appetizers. This seems above and beyond for one man's retirement party but you're not one to start second-guessing a free charcuterie platter. Charcuterie is one of humanity's finest creations. It's just large amounts of meat and cheese presented as though you just randomly found it. It's very easy to eat lots of it without drawing unnecessary attention. Employees around you have already begun to take advantage of the bar and are already loosening up. You've yet to witness a proper company party but from everything you've heard, they're anarchy. Without the infrastructure of the workday and with the addition of alcohol, the natural order of the office is thrown into chaos. A seasoned middle manager could be seen flirting with a new hire. The weak men of accounting might be seen coming to blows in the parking lot, demanding the others to put cigarettes out on their arms so that they can feel something. Mike could become an interesting and sought-after conversation partner. These are all real things from past work parties that you've overheard stories about, though the thing about Mike was told to you by Mike, so it remains dubious. But the rumors have given you an ongoing interest in post-work socialization as well as a persistent fear of the accounting department. The gang is all here. Mike is talking to Tamara, who you now know had a bad day. Meanwhile Gary has already seen a chance to sink his networking claws into upper management and has found The Boss. The two of them are chatting up a middle-aged man in a suit who you can only assume is The Executive. He looks like a bigger, more powerful Gary. After everything the two of you went through today, you're not necessarily eager for more Gary but you can't deny that the man has good business instincts. You didn't come here to chat with coworkers you wouldn't normally chat with. You didn't even *really* come here to congratulate Hank. You came here to get ahead and it's time to start getting the job done. If Gary is jumping into the deep end, then so are you. You approach them, locking your eyes in on Gary, who seems less than thrilled to be losing out on his individualized facetime. But you don't care about Gary anymore. From here on out, the only thing that matters is your career and the happiness its growth will bring you. You enter the conversation with a bang.

Turn to page 152.

'HELLO THERE!'

The version of you that woke up this morning would never have had the courage to socially engage your boss without being first invited into the conversation but that version of you is dead. You've destroyed him to become something new, yet again. The Boss seems surprised and impressed by your bravado. She coolly meets your greeting with a smile and a pause, inviting you to add to this conversation you were so keen on joining.

'I AM REALLY ENJOYING THE PARTY. HOW IS YOUR NIGHT GOING?'

'Well, I can never say no to a good Friday night cocktail,' she says, gesturing with her glass. There appears to be some sort of stick in her drink and in lieu of multiple ice cubes, there is just one singular, incredible cube, so you know it's fancy.

'Or three!' chimes in Gary, trying not to give up an inch of conversational ground.

The Executive laughs a deep, hearty laugh. You can tell just by looking at The Executive that he's never apologized for anything in his life, the true sign of a wealthy man. The Boss sees you and The Executive sussing each other out.

'Oh, you two haven't met yet, this is Jack Hornbach, our CFO if you aren't familiar. Jack, this is one of our rising stars in the design department. He actually started as one of our interns, but he's really been making a splash around here.' It's abundantly clear that The Boss has forgotten your name but you're not the type of employee that'd get hung up on something like that. You're eager to please.

'SUCH A PLEASURE TO MEET YOU SIR. HOW HAS YOUR VISIT BEEN TREATING YOU?'

'Well I never miss a chance to take a trip on the ol' expense account.' He laughs again, relishing the fact that his substantial wealth has also given him access to an expense account full of more wealth. You can't possibly imagine what that feels like. 'Plus, I love to get escorted around the city by this gal. She can keep up with the best of us!' The Boss seems just for a moment to be carrying an exhausted weight in her eyes that you'll never fully know, but it's gone in an instant.

'Jack's in town for the weekend while we finish up some plans for Q4. Speaking of which, are you still clear to come in tomorrow to help out with some odds and ends?'

'OF COURSE, I HAVE NOTHING ELSE PLANNED.'

'Oh perfect, can't go too wild tonight then!' She laughs, as if acknowledging that you have to get up early means you won't actually have to get up early. Gary seems to feel the conversational focus shifting away from him and chimes in.

'I actually can come in tomorrow as well. I had a bar crawl but I'm going to cancel it. I want to make sure I support the team.'

Look at Gary, making plays. Gary's in Sales, there's absolutely no reason for him to come in on a weekend. Yet he's just made himself look like a martyr. On top of that, he's made you look like a nerd by mentioning social activities he's opting not to participate in. You feel like an idiot for making it sound like you were going to spend the weekend sitting quietly in your room with a ham until work began again on Monday, even if that was absolutely your plan.

'Plus, there's no need to go too crazy this weekend, me and my pal here already had ourselves a hell of a lunch today. Isn't that right, bud?'

Good lord, Gary has gone rogue. While there's nothing that says you aren't allowed to eat lunch outside of the office, it's largely considered to be a frivolous use of time that's best left unmentioned. Customarily, a lunch hour is supposed to be cut off at the halfway point by someone who needs help with something they should be able to do on their own. You never dreamed that Gary would disclose this sort of dalliance to a superior and their superior. And you *especially* never believed that he'd disclose said dalliance if it involved both of you getting absolutely covered in wing sauce. This is mutually assured destruction, there's no advantage to sharing this. What could he possibly be playing at? Suddenly it clicks into place.

'I was just gonna have another quiet one at my desk but here comes this guy, all amped up on a Friday afternoon and ready to go to *WING TOWN*, of all places.'

'Is that the chain? The one with the TVs?' The Executive chimes in and you see Gary briefly fight the urge to clarify that while WING TOWN is a chain, each location is encouraged to develop and cultivate its own vibe.

'Yeah, exactly! Anyway, he gets a group together and suddenly we're all having beers and getting into a chicken-wing eating contest in the middle of the day! I protested at first, but I figured hey, the man's got a plan.'

The Boss looks bemused and slightly displeased at the clearly recreational tone of the story currently being told in front of a living business god. She manages the situation as best she can.

'That sounds . . . good for morale.'

'It was! Me and the guys from my department were cracking up. This guy can eat more meat than you could even believe.'

This is a nightmare. Of all your skills, your ability to absolutely crush large quantities of meat is not supposed to be the one being discussed right now. You should've known better than to get involved in Gary's game without a plan. But somehow, The Executive seems amused by the whole story.

'Wow, we've got a champion carnivore here, I guess. Lord, I wish I'd been able to see that. Most of my lunches are green these days. Goddamn doctor says I can't eat red meat.'

'Well c'mon, live vicariously!' Gary gestures toward you. 'Show us your stuff, it's been a few hours, I bet you're hungry again!'

You start to panic.

'OH NO I COULD NOT POSSIBLY, THERE AREN'T EVEN CHICKEN WINGS HERE.' You kick yourself: you have no idea what the chicken-wing situation at this party is.

'Well we can improvise!' Gary says, moving over the appetizer table and grabbing a charcuterie platter. It's covered in various meats. Just the smell as it approaches is nearly enough to make you salivate. You hate that Gary is doing this to you, but moreover you hate that he's right about how hungry you are. 'C'mon, just give us a taste, polish this bad boy off!'

By making this into a whole thing, Gary has put you on the spot. He's going to keep pushing until you either say no and potentially create an awkward lull in conversation or say yes, eating so much meat that neither The Boss or The Executive could ever possibly respect you. You either need to defuse the situation or confidently eat this charcuterie platter and you need to do it quickly.

If you wish to play Gary's game and get into your second meat-based spectacle of the day, turn to page 157.

If you wish to have some self-respect and decline, no matter the cost, turn to page 171.

YOU'VE COME THIS FAR. One day, a wolf walked out of the woods and decided to be a man. And now here you are, one personal debasement away from moderately amusing the wealthy people who employ you. It sickens you that you're considering doing this just to get Gary off your back. After everything the two of you went through today, you thought that at the very least he'd leave you alone, but that assumption feels foolish now. You stare at the meat tray as Gary holds it toward you and you hate that it looks appealing. Sure, the meat will be delicious, but this is about more than meat. This is about dignity and the respect of mid-tier executives who don't remember most of their employees' names. It hits you that maybe you've been playing this all wrong. You chose business tonight. You chose to skip your date and come to a work function with almost no non-work-related social value. So why are you approaching these people as though you're friends with them? Corporate America is just as ruthless as the woods; the only difference is everyone is wearing pants. So maybe it's time to bring some ferocity back into your life and attack Gary just when he thinks he's winning. He may be trying to embarrass you by discussing your meat prowess, but he was in that contest too. In fact . . .

'GARY IS BEING MODEST SIR. HE ACTUALLY WON THE CONTEST TODAY, I CAME IN A PALTRY SECOND PLACE.'

Brilliant. Now Gary either has to admit that he's just as much of a meat eater as you or lie and say he didn't win, something a man as competitive as him could never bring himself to do. The Executive takes the bait.

'Is that true, Gary?'

'Well, I mean, yeah sure, but it was more of a fluke than—'

Incredible, he was too competitive to lie and now he's fallen into his own trap. Gary created a world where it seemed obvious that the man who can eat the most meat should demonstrate that skill and then accidentally admitted to being the man that could eat the most meat.

'SO HONORABLE, THIS MODESTY. GARY IS AN INCRED-IBLE LITTLE MEAT BOY, HE WOULD BE MUCH MORE ENTERTAINING TO WATCH THAN ME.'

Gary uses diminutive terms like 'buddy' and 'champ' to make everyone sound like his son and establish dominance. You assume that referring to Gary as a 'little meat boy' will have the same effect.

'His logic's sound, Gary, looks like you've got a meat plate to polish off.'

'Oh, sir, I'm actually still a bit full up from earlier, maybe in a bit.'

Gary is looking around nervously and visibly sweating. People nearby have begun to take notice of the situation. You could care less what this does to Gary's reputation in the office. Gary chose to mess with you and you're no longer in the business of friendship. You're in the business of business and tonight you're making sure Gary never sticks his nose in yours again. You underline the rules of this game.

'EAT THE PLATTER, GARY. BE THE LITTLE MEAT BOY.'

The look Gary gives you would make any man feel a chill down his spine, but you're not a goddamn man. You're something darker and worse and right now you're brimming with power. Gary takes a piece of meat off the platter, places it in his mouth, and begins to chew. It's boring you.

'C'MON EAT MORE, LITTLE MEAT BOY.'

Maybe you're going a little hard on the whole 'little meat boy' thing but then The Executive starts to say it too. And so do your coworkers. Before too long, the whole room has turned its attention to Gary with a chant of 'LITTLE MEAT BOY, LITTLE MEAT BOY' and with each passing chant, Gary shovels more and more meat into his mouth. He's sweating bullets, physically uncomfortable, but he keeps eating more and more until he pitches forward with a yelp. He doubles over and vomits a little onto the floor. He stands up in silence, a tiny puddle of puke at his feet. He turns to The Boss.

'I think . . . I think I need to go ho—'

An onslaught of ham leaves Gary's mouth, hitting The Boss and the entire front of her shirt. The room is in chaos suddenly as everyone takes a step back, worried about where the little meat boy will vomit next. But he's defeated and has no plans to stay. Gary turns tail and sprints out the front door of Corb. Will you ever see him again? You wouldn't blame him for leaving town. But as far as you're concerned, he got everything he deserved. The Boss quickly rushes off to the bathroom to clean herself up and everyone tries to act like everything is normal until a supervisor tells them how to react to this new piece of gossip. As everyone returns to their conversation, you feel a tap on your shoulder and turn to find The Executive.

'I've gotta say, that was impressive. It's a bit of a mess in here though, how about we grab a cigar on the roof?'

A personal invitation to one-on-one time with The Executive? There's never been an easier choice for you to make. You follow him to the elevator, and he leads you out to a rooftop deck where he hands you a cigar. You let it just sort of sit in your mouth, trying to avoid the absolutely horrific smell, taste, and texture of this expensive thing. The city looks beautiful at night. You've never seen it like this, as these views are usually reserved for high rollers. And now, it seems, you.

'I hate all the ass-kissers you meet on trips like this. You're a breath of fresh air my friend. The way you just absolutely humiliated that guy, it was beautiful.'

'OH, THANK YOU. GARY SUCKS.'

The Executive laughs, 'Yeah, there's a Gary in every office. They sniff out that we're looking for new managers and think that embarrassing stunts like that are going to get him considered. Poor guy thinks his career is going places.'

'OH, IS HE GOING TO GET FIRED FOR BEING SUCH A LITTLE MEAT BOY?'

'Not a chance! You keep a guy like that around and he's yours to command for a good twenty–thirty years. We'll keep him right where he is. You, however . . . you're going places.'

'OH AM I?' This is news to you. You hope the places are good.

'Modest too, I love it!' The Executive is talking to you like a peer now. 'Listen kid, a guy like you sitting in an entry-level position is a waste. I'm not trying to tell tales out of school here but we're hiring a new manager for your office. I know we just met, but a man as ruthless as you is going to be useful in a boardroom.'

'WAIT, SO I WOULD BE THE BOSS?'

'Buddy, you'd be your boss's boss. I know potential when I see it.'

The Executive aggressively puffs smoke toward the skyline and gazes out over the river below.

'You could get used to this, right? Bigger salary, better benefits, corner office. Whattya say?'

This job could change everything. Managers have their own offices and almost no oversight. You'd likely never have your identity challenged by a coworker again purely out of fear. Ostensibly this is everything you wanted when you came here. Stability, flexibility, and the blind acceptance of an entire group of people based purely on your income. This job could finally make you one of them, one of the important people. Saying yes should be obvious, but at the pit of your stomach, you feel the faintest knot.

If you accept a massive, unearned promotion, turn to page 163.

If you follow your gut and say no, turn to page 168.

ONE YEAR LATER

'TELL ME, WOLF, why should I trust you?'

You'd be sweating if you could. You're sitting across the table from Jacob Horne, a man of untold wealth and you need to get him to sign this contract. Horne's a notoriously tough negotiator, but you have your eyes fixed on your prey. You pace toward Horne, arms behind your back. You'd take a moment to congratulate yourself on how good you've become at corporate posturing but frankly it's all old hat to you now. You know Horne wants to sign the contract because the contract will make him money. He's just making you sing for your supper. But you don't sing. You scream.

'BECAUSE WE BOTH KNOW WHAT THIS IS ABOUT, HORNE.'

'Oh do we?'

You just said that you do but you've picked up that half of the drama of business meetings comes from repeating the last thing someone said. 'YES, WE DO.'

'Well, do tell me what I'm missing here.'

'CONSIDER SKELETONS.'

You've got his attention now.

'WHEN YOU SEE A SKELETON SOMEWHERE, IS IT IN A GROUP?'

Silence. They're all yours.

'NO, MY FRIENDS. THEY ARE ALWAYS ALONE. SKELE- TONS ARE SKELETONS BECAUSE THEY ARE DEAD AND THEY ARE DEAD BECAUSE THEY DID NOT HAVE ENOUGH BUSINESS ASSOCIATES. THOSE ARE THE FACTS. THOSE THAT WANDER ALONE TEND TO DIE ALONE. BUT TO- GETHER, NOTHING CAN STOP US. DEATH CAN'T COME FOR OUR FORTUNES. MONEY IS FOREVER. TOGETHER, LET US NEVER BECOME SKELETONS.'

The room bursts into applause. Your metaphor didn't make a lot of sense, but you've learned that the key to crushing a meeting like this is easy: just be higher ranking than everyone else. As it turns out, you can say just about anything when you sign the checks. Horne looks you dead in the eye.

'Let's do some business, my friend.'

He scribbles his signature on the contract in front of him. Then he stands up, walks up to you, and shakes your paw.

'Together, we'll triple the price of insulin.'

'BUDDY, I WON'T REST UNTIL IT'S QUADRUPLED.'

The two of you share a big, performative business laugh. You walk out of the conference room with purpose. You've just sealed a gigantic business deal and if you slow down for even a second, one of your many admirers is likely to try to talk to you before you can get back to your office. When the guys at corporate hear about this, they're going to flip. You walk down the hall toward your corner office when suddenly Gary approaches you.

'Hey, hey boss, just heard the good news. Sounds like you were incredible in there!'

'NOT NOW, LITTLE MEAT BOY.'

You keep walking but Gary stops, crestfallen. You'd feel bad for him if you didn't call him that every day. You're quickly flanked by your intern. You haven't bothered to learn his name; he just brings you various beverages throughout the day. This time is no different. He hands you a coffee, but you lose your step for a moment and bump into him, spilling the hot drink on the floor. It splashes up onto your perfectly pressed suit.

'OH MY GOD YOU ABSOLUTE CHODE.'

'I am SO sorry Mr. Wolf, I'll get you some towels from—'

'GET YOURSELF SOME TOWELS IN HELL, YOU'RE FIRED.'

Just like that he's gone, vanished down the hallway in a stunned silence. You strut past your assistant into your office.

'BRETT, MOVE MY AFTERNOON MEETING. THIS RE-CENTLY UNEMPLOYED ASS GOT COFFEE ON MY SHIRT.'

You shut the door behind you and draw the blinds to your office. You drop back down to four legs, sitting in front of your window and looking out upon your incredible corner-office view. Landing the Horne contract should feel like a win, but it doesn't. Nothing has lately and you're unsure why. Once you got promoted, every-thing got easier. You got an office and all the private time that allows. You were given more money than you'll ever know what to do with, and on top of it all, you were given the greatest safety net of all for your secret: power. You eat your rotisserie chickens in public now. You tell people to call you Wolf. Hell, you can shake hands now. Any one of these things would've ruined you a year ago and yet here you are. As it turns out, having money and power means that nobody pays much mind to who you are or what you're hiding. In fact, beyond your money and power, they hardly care about you at all. You find yourself accepted but alone. Your complete embrace of corporate culture has brought you success but no one to share it with. You could chase after another promotion, and even another after that, but you wonder if the praise of these sycophants has any hope of quieting the dull hum of loneliness in your heart.

Brett knocks on the door.

'COME IN.'

'Sorry sir, I know you wanted some time to clean up but corporate is on the line and I thought you'd want to give them the good news yourself.'

You don't bother standing up.

'ARE WE FRIENDS, BRETT?'

'I'm sorry sir?'

'WE'VE KNOWN EACH OTHER FOR QUITE AWHILE. WE'VE SPENT TIME TOGETHER AT CHICKEN-WING RESTAURANTS. ARE WE FRIENDS?'

'I'm not sure I understand the question, sir. Is there something I can get for you?'

'JUST DIAL ME INTO THE CALL.'

Brett shuts the door behind him as he leaves. The phone rings. You sigh. It rings again.

————

CONGRATULATIONS! You've ruthlessly ascended the corporate ladder and been rewarded with power, influence, and an existential crisis that will haunt you for the remainder of your life! Pour yourself a whiskey and stare out your office window, pal, you're a real human now!

THE END.

YOU ALWAYS DREAMED that someday someone would think you were good enough at your job to promote you. You always felt that being promoted would represent true assimilation with mankind and even though you've had your doubts and anxieties about it, you've been confident on some level that it would happen. You just never expected it to feel too easy. You're only here because of a simple charcuterie platter and some light workplace intrigue. You didn't prove your worth with incredible levels of productivity or by sealing a big business deal. You're just here because you made Gary look like a fool in a way that amused your boss's boss. Embarrassing Gary downstairs was fun but it's not who you are. You don't want to have to regularly indulge your worst impulses just to secure your own place in the world. This promotion must be an aberration. The system is supposed to reward merit, not the whims of wealthy executives.

'I'M SORRY SIR BUT I HAVE TO RESPECTFULLY DECLINE.'

You'd always wanted to be able to say that in a business setting, but it brings you no joy right now. Jack pauses for a second and really looks you over. You're worried maybe he's on to you. Perhaps his offer was too good for any human man to pass up.

'Oh, so it's my job you're after, you little shit?'

Nope, he's just regular business angry.

'NO SIR, I JUST DON'T THINK THE PROMOTION WILL BE A GOOD FIT FOR ME.'

Jack steps up closer to you and pokes his finger into your chest aggressively.

'Listen kid, I don't know what you're playing at here but it's not gonna work. You can't hardball this, you're getting my best offer. Frankly you're lucky I even gave it. We were going to spend the weekend interviewing candidates for this job, but I thought maybe I'd save us all some trouble. But I guess you're just stupid.'

'NO SIR, I UNDERSTAND, I JUST DO NOT WANT THIS JOB.'

'So, you're just an ingrate, then? Or what, are you not ready for a big-boy job? God, you young people are all so goddamn lazy.'

Suddenly, as you look at Jack, he comes into focus. You see who he really is, despite all the work he does to hide it. He's weak. A selfish, aging man with nothing to throw around but the arbitrary power afforded to him by a game already rigged in his favor. He's a man who sees his personal comfort as the only important cause on the planet and it's made him pathetic. Jack just tries to drown out the chaos around him with expensive suits and cigars. This is a man who has everything and chooses to do nothing of substance. But you won't be controlled. You're not a man like Jack. You're not a man at all. You're a goddamn wolf. You lean in close and bark in Jack's face. His face goes white as a sheet as he realizes all at once that he's just failed to justify his future at the company. He tries to step back from you but falls onto the ground. You drop down on all fours and pounce, sinking your teeth into his femoral artery. It's a symphony of blood and viscera. In moments, Jack goes from mid-tier executive to charcuterie platter. You take your time and dig into your dinner. You take in the view of the city, its orange hued lights shining out over a busy but serene Friday evening. The full moon casts an eerie glow over all of it, inviting you to speculate on your place in this city's future. Perhaps you've doomed yourself. Or perhaps Jack could sit on the VIP-only rooftop deck for hours before anyone with the clearance to find him would come looking. You could make a quiet exit and sleep soundly tonight. Getting a full night's rest is important. You volunteered to go into work tomorrow and you want to make an impression. After all, an upper management position has just opened up.

———————

You ate the rich! Congratulations! Your inability to stomach a world run by mid-tier executives has led you to an uncertain future but a clear conscience. But good luck paying the rent with that!

THE END.

YOU DID *NOT* LEAVE THE WOODS to be forced to eat stale meat in public by a man as weak as Gary. He may not ever be able to know it, but you are his superior in every way. You could tear him limb from limb without even thinking and every moment you resist the urge to do so should be treated as though he's received mercy from the heavens themselves. You are not beholden to Gary's power games any longer and it's time to let him know that.

'I'M SORRY GARY BUT I'M NOT GOING TO DO THAT.'

Predictably, Gary was prepared for this answer.

'Aw c'mon man, it'll be funny! Everybody wants to see, right?' Gary looks to The Boss, who rolls her eyes and seems embarrassed by this whole spectacle, but much to your chagrin you see that The Executive nods with a smile plastered across his face.

'I'd really *love* to see this.'

'Hear that pal, you can't let Jack down while he's on vacation!'

'GARY, I DO NOT WANT TO EAT THAT MEAT.'

'Seriously man, you're gonna leave us all hanging like this?'

Now Gary has decided to spin this like it's some sort of thing you offered to do that you're now backing out of. But you're going to hold firm no matter what happens. You think it may be a good idea to take the moral high ground here.

'SERIOUSLY GARY I DO NOT WANT TO EAT THAT WHOLE PLATTER, I WOULD REALLY APPRECIATE IF—'

Gary steps in a bit closer, just barely edging into what you'd consider your personal space and almost involuntarily you yell even louder than usual,

'GET THE FUCK AWAY FROM ME, GARY.'

You turn abruptly and accidentally knock the platter out of Gary's hands. It clatters onto the floor loudly and the room falls silent. You've made a critical error.

Interpersonal conflict at an office party is like blood in the water. Everyone has taken notice and now this incident will define Monday's gossip. While it was good to be clear about your boundaries and stand up for yourself, this appears to be another of those times when self-respect is better in concept than in execution. You upheld your personal boundaries, sure, but you also made an above average level of noise, forgetting an important rule of human socialization: it's better for one's reputation to be degraded quietly than to stand up for yourself loudly. Corporate America was practically founded on this principle and you just pissed all over it. You're a damn fool. You have to try and save face.

'HAHA JUST KIDDING PAL, I WILL EAT THE MEAT.'

You crouch down to the floor and begin to eat capicola ham off the ground to prove how chill you can be.

'I THINK IT'S FUN AND THIS WAS MY IDEA! WE ALL WANTED THIS AND WE LOVE IT, RIGHT FRIENDS?'

They aren't buying it. The Boss shakes her head and looks down while Gary feigns confusion as if to say, 'How could this awkward situation I forced into existence have possibly come to pass?' The Executive has the bemused look on this face of a man who gets to fly far away from this town in three days. You try to look at them pleadingly but receive nothing in return. In fact, no one will even meet your gaze. The room has already turned on you without question. You've drawn attention to yourself and until these people's superiors tell them how they're supposed to feel about that, you're in exile. You've ruined everything. You've never had this much attention on you for this long, but you can only assume that if you stay here, the screaming will be what starts next. You sheepishly lift your head up from the meat pile on the floor, hoping that maybe your coworkers will just agree to forget about this and all turn back around, returning to their conversations about the latest HBO shows. But they all watch as you slowly, nearly silently, take one more quick bite of floor ham. The second it's in your mouth, someone begins to scream.

'That's a fucking wolf!'

'SORRY, SORRY, I'M SORRY, IT'S JUST REALLY GOOD HAM! I'M JUST A GUY, I PROMISE!'

Then you are sprinting, still on all fours, through the crowd. As you propel yourself toward the door, you see Mike, in some asinine attempt at heroism, trying to block you from reaching it. You have no idea why Mike thinks that keeping a live wolf trapped inside a corporate event will make him look good, but you can't let him stand in your way. You briefly suss out Mike's many vulnerable areas; you could destroy him in seconds. But for some reason you can't bring yourself to end him, even if he is a big, boring, idiot. This man isn't like Gary. Gary you'd have taken pleasure in eating. Mike is simply trying to survive. Perhaps in a different world you'd have seen that sooner and found a way to become his friend. Ideally in that parallel world, Mike also doesn't say 'awesome-sauce' anymore. As he stands trembling between you and the door, you disarm Mike in the most empathetic way you can.

'IT WAS ME, MIKE. I WAS THE ONE EATING YOUR LUNCHES.'

He looks at you in shock before his shoulders sink down and his gaze drops to the floor, ' . . . I guess I always knew.'

Bullshit Mike, you were acting like the goddamn Sherlock Holmes of pasta theft not even twelve hours ago. But you let him have this. Just as his vulnerability briefly overtakes him, you lunge at him, knocking him to the ground, unharmed. You fly past him and out the door. There's no hope for you in this world and you feel like an idiot for having ever thought that there was. You run out onto the sidewalk, where you quickly duck into an alley before you can draw too much attention to yourself. You pop back up on two feet and dust yourself off a bit, though you're not sure why. After what happened in there, your coworkers are certain to be at least somewhat suspicious that you aren't what you say you are. You're pretty sure one of them even used the word 'wolf' specifically. But as you walk back out into the street, you're unsure of where you'll go next. The idea of returning to the woods seems mortifying. Your family would probably mock you to no end for thinking that you could find a better life where you didn't belong. They'd never understand what it feels like to be in your position. But maybe you don't need to make a decision right away. Sure, there's no going back to work, but you seem to have re-assimilated yourself into this Friday night fairly seamlessly. You feel yourself at a great crossroads with no clear path and if that's the direction your life is going, you don't see any harm in partaking in one final human rite of passage: sulking in a dark bar.

———

To sulk in a dark bar, turn to page 176.

YOU'VE NEVER BEEN IN A REAL BAR. You've been inside plenty of places that serve alcohol, but the idea of an alcohol-exclusive location always seemed unwise to you as someone whose kidneys weren't made to process it. All this time spent trying to survive as a human and you still feel like you never properly got to live as one. Everything you did was always so cautious, perfectly calculated to make sure that it wouldn't bother anyone or even draw their attention. In the woods it had felt like a different shade of the same. You'd overcommitted yourself, confidently and defiantly, in an attempt to hide the fact that you were never really sure about what you were doing or if you wanted to be doing it at all. It frustrates and worries you to think that of all the places you've tried to fit in; none have had a place for you. But at least you're in the right head-space for your first trip to a dark bar. You see a humble-looking building with a neon 'OPEN' sign and a few slightly wobbly individuals smoking cigarettes outside. You've always thought cigarettes looked extremely cool, but you have a whole different lip situation than humans so sadly they're something you have to watch from afar. The bar is called Ed & Jane's. It's perfect. You walk inside and are immediately confronted with an olfactory overload. The air is sour and musty, with a slightly degraded version of cigarette smoke hanging in it. You'd imagine that this place would smell strongly even to someone whose nose wasn't incredibly powerful. The light is dim, but not dark. The entire place feels wonderfully free from time by some sort of mutual agreement from its patrons, who talk mostly amongst themselves and quietly so as not to distract anyone from their booze-based task at hand. The crowd is light, but you assume that as the Friday evening progresses, it's bound to grow. You post up at the bar, a near perfect height to balance yourself on. The bartender gives you a single look, with eye contact and all.

'A BIG CHEAP BEER, PLEASE,' you say, not feeling like you need to convince anyone that you've had a long day.

Without missing a beat, the bartender pours you a big beer in a glass mug. When he turns his back to you, you lap up a few quick mouthfuls of a beverage that had until just now been only aspirational for you. It doesn't taste the way you thought it would. It doesn't taste like anything you can think of. Frankly, it's a little terrible, but it makes your ears feel warm and everything that happened at Corb stops replaying so loudly in your mind. You exhale and feel yourself relax. You definitely see the appeal. Suddenly, a man pulls out the stool directly next to you and sits down. There are other stools available in the bar, so his choice to sit in your close proximity is a distressing one. This man is either already drunk, looking to make small talk, or both. He orders a beer as well and turns toward you, and that's when you realize. It's Hank.

'You must've been having as bad a time at that thing as I was.'

'HAHA YEAH THAT WAS NOT AN IDEAL SOCIAL ENVIR-
ONMENT FOR ME. GOOD TO SEE YOU HANK. HEY, JUST
OUT OF CURIOSITY WHEN DID YOU LEAVE CORB?'

'Pretty much as soon as there were enough people there for me
to slip out without attracting any attention. I've been here for over
an hour now. Turns out that I think those parties are bullshit even
when they're throwing one for me.'

'OH, SO YOU DIDN'T SEE ANY SORT OF MEAT NIGHT-
MARE?'

'What?'

'NOTHING, INCREDIBLY COOL. I HATE PARTIES TOO
WHICH IS WHY I LEFT, THERE WAS NO NIGHTMARE.'

Hank laughs, 'Nah, I get it man, you're right. Those things *are* a
nightmare.' He takes a big long sip of his beer. 'They don't care that
I'm retiring, I've said maybe ten non-work sentences, collectively,
to that entire office.'

'OH NO I'M SURE THEY CARE ABOUT YOU A LOT.'

'Nah, The Boss just wanted to impress that guy from corporate.
I guarantee, if that guy wasn't in town it would've been a box of
baked goods in the breakroom and her briefly forgetting how to
pronounce my last name. So, why'd you leave?'

You try improvise a quick lie. 'UGH, GARY WAS BEING—'

'God, *fuck* that guy. That whole company is designed to chew
people up and spit them out looking like him. The only kind of
people that succeed the way he has are the ones who are willing to
lick any boot or stab any back to get ahead. He's morally bankrupt
and boring on top of that. The man's a waste of a good jawline.
Whatever that guy said to you, don't let it get in your head.'

You've never heard someone so blatantly disparage a coworker before and can't help but feel like it's a trap of some kind. Usually you'd bad mouth a coworker by saying one or two nice things followed by one really bad one to test the waters. And then, and only then, if the person you were talking to agreed, you'd launch into your true feelings. And no matter what you'd close the conversation with some sort of neutral rejoinder like, 'Love the guy though.'

'HAHA YEAH GARY IS NOT GREAT.'

'Well, whatever that moron did, I'm selfishly glad to at least have a little company.' He raises his mug and clinks it into yours. 'Us outsiders gotta stick together, am I right?'

Wait, what does he mean by that?

'I ACTUALLY HAVE ALWAYS REALLY FELT LIKE A PART OF THE FAMILY AT THE OFFICE, I LOVE THAT WE—'

Hank cuts you off, 'C'mon man. You don't have to do the whole spiel, it's just us.'

What does Hank know?

'Relax. I'm just saying you aren't like them. You try to be, but you aren't. I'm not either! I split early from the last interaction I'll ever have with those people just because I couldn't stand to sit through another forced conversation. It's okay. God knows I tried to be one of them at your age, just like you are.'

'AND IT NEVER WORKED?'

The question slipped out of you as quickly as the thought entered your mind. You're sure the beer is playing some role in this, but you've also never talked to someone like Hank. Your interactions have always been dominated by a very deliberate pacing and language to make sure that neither party misunderstood the other or thought that the other person was weird. Your conversations have often felt like transactions in pursuit of some mundane end. You're not sure you've ever talked to someone who just wants to talk before.

'Nah, not in the way I wanted. Their whole thing, where you get the job, then you get married, then you get the bigger job, it just never . . . took, I guess. I never wanted it like they did.'

'DOESN'T THAT MAKE YOU SAD?'

'Maybe sometimes. But overall? I don't think so. I've got hobbies, friends I see when I can, my life's not some non-stop thrill ride but whose is, y'know?'

'BUT WHY IS IT SO EASY FOR ALL OF THEM?'

'Honestly? Who knows? I could rant about how they're all sheep and I'm some big genius but I'm not any better or worse than they are, I'm just different. They all seem to approach every day in that place with this big, bright optimism. Like they're so excited to be exactly where they are, and I've never felt that way. And the hard part is that they're nice! Most of them are fine people! But I can't seem to return whatever energy it is they try to give me, so I either have to reject it or I have to fake it or I try to be myself around them and I end up making them feel uncomfortable. Maybe I was supposed to do something else or maybe I'm just an asshole. But friendship with somebody who I can't speak with freely feels hollow. Enough years of that and you end up learning how to entertain yourself. The way I see it, the world doesn't work for everybody, but we're all stuck here. Some people love their jobs, they fit in, and they don't think about it too much. I'm not that guy. But I'd never make it through the day if I let that make me sad. The idea of being that guy is what makes me sad, and I'm sure that if I were that guy, the idea of being me would make me sad. I figure I'm exactly who I'm supposed to be, even if it's not always a cakewalk.'

Wow, bars rule.

'But it seems like you're getting at something here, what's eating you?'

'NOTHING COULD EAT ME HOW FUCKING DARE YOU.' Oh wow this beer is doing quick work. Hank laughs.

'You know what I mean man, it's obvious that this whole thing is bothering you. You talk like somebody twice your age. You've had a quarter of a beer and we're already ranting about being lonely so spill it, what happened in there?'

You briefly consider pointing out that Hank was the one to bring up loneliness first, but this doesn't seem like the time or place. At first, the thought that Hank had missed out on your grand humiliation felt like a second chance. Obviously, the sensible decision would be to pretend that the party never happened and to move on, find a new job, and appreciate your good luck. But Hank really got to you just then. The little void he described feels like your own. The isolation you fear so desperately, he celebrates. Maybe he's right, and there's no point in trying to become some perfect model of a human man and instead the only times you can know you're truly alive are when someone can see as full a picture of you as you're able to give.

'HANK, I'M A WOLF.'

Hank's eyes widen and he stares at you. It should feel invasive or dangerous, telling someone your secret like this but he doesn't stare with suspicion or fear. He's just looking at you. As though he's been given context that's sent everything about you clicking into place. You wait with a pit in your stomach, worried that soon you'll be chased out of here or worse. Hank nods.

'Nice.'

That's it? You're thrilled to not be dealing with yet another screaming person but frankly you feel like the reveal of your entire identity merits a bit more than just a simple 'Nice' but beggars can't be choosers.

'YOU HEARD WHAT I SAID?'

'Yeah. You're a wolf.'

'YEAH LIKE ONE OF THE BIG ONES.'

'Makes sense. I mean obviously I have questions, but I don't want to overwhelm you. I mean . . . how?'

You explain everything you can to Hank. You explain how you left the woods, fled into the city, found an apartment, and learned how to delicately hold a mug. Hank just listens and nods.

'Goddamn,' he says, polishing off his beer, 'that's impressive as hell.'

Well if Hank isn't going to make a big deal out of it, you won't either. You look around the bar at its various patrons, all engrossed in their own conversation or lack of conversation, and allow yourself to be pleased for a moment. Hank knows your secret, but nothing has changed. He just understands you a bit more and in turn you understand him a bit more. There's no stress, no fear, just a moment to recognize that you've had a very good Friday night against all odds.

'SO, WHAT SHOULD WE DO NOW?'

'How about a shot of whiskey?'

'OH, WOW I'M GOING TO BE HONEST WITH YOU HANK, I HAVE NEVER HAD IT BEFORE AND I'M FAIRLY CONCERNED ABOUT MY INTERNAL ORGANS.'

'Hey that makes two of us, pal. I'm not gonna twist your arm over it but if we can't celebrate right now, when can we?'

Hank has a point. After everything that's transpired today, you certainly deserve to be able to relax a bit. And so far, the half of a beer that you've consumed has only made the night more enjoyable. You feel energetic, but in control of your actions. Maybe it's time to start being a little less cautious in your day-to-day life and start enjoying some good old-fashioned human impulsiveness. Plus, you like talking to Hank and you like how chill he is about the whole thing of you in fact being a very large predatory beast wearing a tie. You'd hate to squander what could very well blossom into a valuable friendship. But you'd also hate to throw up on that same friend.

If you think it's time to try whiskey out for the first time, turn to page 185.

If you prefer to err on the side of caution, turn to page 190.

YOU KNOW WHAT? You've earned this. You've spent so much time hectoring yourself for small missteps, it's time to cut into the actual joy of living. Tonight is a big night for you. You've opened up to a fellow human being and found acceptance, you've forced yourself out of a job that didn't actually value you, and now you're going to enjoy a goddamn drink of alcohol.

'YOU KNOW WHAT HANK, YEAH, LET'S GO FOR IT.'

Hank smiles, 'That's the spirit!' he says before motioning for the bartender. 'Two shots of Horrid Hound, we're making a night of it!'

The waitress brings the shots over in their tiny, clear glasses. As she clinks them down on the bar, you nearly brim over with excitement. Hank clinks his glass into yours, doing you the distinct favor of not making you balance a tiny shot glass between two paws, and makes a toast.

'To unexpected friends.'

'TO UNEXPECTED FRIENDS!' You lap up the shot from the glass and immediately your taste buds are under attack. The combination of whiskey's smell and taste makes you retch backward and exhale harshly. You steady yourself against the bar, unable to imagine how anyone could possibly enjoy doing that. Then just seconds later, you are a being free of pain. Suddenly, there's not a single thing in the world that could stop you from having a great night. There's a dull humming in your ears. In fact, all your senses seem to be slightly impaired, but for once you find yourself exceptionally open to the idea of just going with the flow. The next thing you know, you and Hank are laughing, and you can't remember what about. You're consuming a second shot, but this one doesn't hurt like the first. It just makes you feel like you have no physical presence at all. In fact, you hadn't even noticed that you've fallen down onto the floor. Falling down in a public place is ostensibly a bad thing, but right now it feels like a good thing. Hank looks worried as he helps you up but you're fine. You try to tell him you're fine, but your words don't seem to come out right. You wriggle out of his grasp, trying to help yourself up but you slide back to the sticky barroom floor. It's fine down here, you think, but suddenly there are lots of other hands on you. You try to tell everyone not to worry and stand up on your own but the humming in your ears has gotten so loud. Your mind flits in and out of coherence, like you're bobbing above water and then suddenly, it all goes warm and dark.

Turn to page 187.

OPENING YOUR EYES HURTS. There's light everywhere and each individual sunbeam is a personal attack on your well-being. You can tell your eyes are working but you'd call what you're experiencing less 'sight' and more 'a series of laser beams to the eyes', but slowly shapes start to form and come into focus. You're at your apartment. You even made it into your bedroom. Your head hurts and you feel tired even though you were just asleep. You're still wearing your work clothes, though they feel wet. You don't want to stick around long enough to discover why your bed is wet. Plus, your body is absolutely screaming for water, so you have bigger things to focus on right now. You walk out into the living room, prepared to bark some sort of brief excuse at Caleb but he doesn't appear to be home. You try to think of how any of this happened, but you're completely missing any sort of memories of last night. Maybe you were poisoned. Gary? Did Gary poison you? That's when you see the clock. It's already 11:30. You've completely overslept the week-end work meetings you were supposed to attend. You've likely completely tanked your reputation with your boss and it might have even cost you your job. You're distraught. You'd run into the office right now and try to fix this, but you look like hell. Your fur is matted and sticky for some reason and it appears as though you got covered in vomit somehow. There also appears to be a dark, sticky substance in your coat that you'd assume was blood if you weren't so sure that you had just been quietly sleeping in your room. Maybe you got into Caleb's leftover borscht again? You walk over to the fridge to find an absolute mess of human remains on the kitchen floor. You are not underselling when you say that this may be the most shredded up you've ever seen a person; you really feasted with reckless abandon here. You're working on the assumption that this mess is not Caleb's borscht. It would seem that this time, the borscht is Caleb.

Your body's inability to process alcohol didn't go away just because it contextually seemed like it should. You ate your roommate and blacked out on one of the most important conversations you've ever had. And now you've overslept and are late for work. Your story is over.

YOU HAVE NO DOUBT that drinking whiskey would probably be fun. It'd be a thrilling new experience that could open up incalculable other, newer, experiences for you. But it could also go horribly wrong. Even though it feels like a good time to experiment, you know that your body's unpredictable alcohol tolerance doesn't care much about context. A bad idea doesn't become less of a bad idea even if it starts to *sound* like more fun.

'I'M SORRY HANK BUT I JUST DON'T THINK TONIGHT IS A WHISKEY NIGHT.'

Hank doesn't give it a second thought. 'Say no more! Won't be the first or last time I've taken a shot alone,' he says, gesturing for the bartender. She pours him a shot which he raises toward you. 'To unexpected friends!'

'TO UNEXPECTED FRIENDS,' you say along with him, quietly taking a few more laps of your nearly untouched beer once the bartender leaves you. This feels like all the alcohol you'll need for tonight. It seems as though Hank is in the same boat. His movements are a bit more frenetic now. Hank stares off into space, either thinking or maybe just a little drunk.

'I'm gonna be honest man, I can't believe I'm done with that company. I never thought the day would come.'

'IT MUST FEEL GOOD TO HAVE MORE TIME TO YOUR-SELF.'

'It does. I'm lucky, I got paid well, I just can't help but think . . .'

Hank trails off. He takes a sip of his beer and turns around to you with intensity in his eyes.

'I gave that place the best years of my life. I always told myself I was above it, and that I didn't define myself by what happened at that place. It was just a paycheck. But I've gotta be honest man, it pisses me off to go out so quietly. They're a few blocks away at MY going away party and I bet none of them have even realized that I left.'

He has a point. Even before your accidental unveiling brought the evening to a screeching halt, Hank's party seemed to have shockingly little to do with Hank. It makes you sad to think that a place that cares so little about its people holds so much sway over their lives. Just this morning you would've counted yourself a member of their office family. But now you're starting to understand that humanity contains a lot of the same brutal, emotionless machinations you'd seen in the woods. There's just more effort put into dressing them up.

'IT'S NOT FAIR THAT THEY CAN BEHAVE THIS WAY.'

Speaking ill of the company fills you with a nervous exhilaration, the light tinge of excitement in having sinned against your now dead god. Hank is really into it.

'It's not!'

'THEY CAN'T JUST USE PEOPLE UP AND THROW THEM AWAY.'

'Yeah!'

'I WISH SOMEONE WOULD DESTROY THAT PLACE!'

Hank goes silent and looks you directly in the eyes.

'You're absolutely right,' he says, reaching hastily into his pocket and pulling out his work key card. 'How much do you wanna bet that this thing still works? Office is open to staff twenty-four-seven so that we can all impress each other with how much sleep we lose working late but the whole office is down the road kissing corporate ass right now. You know what that means?'

'WHAT DOES IT MEAN?'

Hank downs the last of his drink and sets it down on the bar. He hastily stands up and starts putting on his coat. He throws some cash down on the bar.

'It means we're gonna go put in some unpaid overtime.'

Turn to page 193.

THE TWO OF YOU ENCOUNTER absolutely no resistance getting back into the office. After all, who would want to stop two intrepid and somewhat drunk employees from giving their Friday night back to the company that so graciously provided in the first place? You exit the elevator to find everything just as you'd suspected. The office is fully lit but empty. The only sound is the soft droning of the fluorescent lights. Hank saunters around with a wild look in his eye, like he doesn't know where to start. You trot around on all fours without fear once you get out of the elevator, sniffing around. Suddenly Hank stops at a desk. Specifically, at Gary's desk. Hank can barely hide his contempt as he looks at Gary's immaculate workspace. It's adorned with a bulletin board bearing an inspirational quote from a movie he likely hasn't watched. In front of his computer sits a metallic sculpture of a shark that's supposed to represent something business-related. Hank shakes his head laughing and finally looks down at the exercise ball that Gary calls a chair. He grabs the metal shark, holds it in his hand for a moment, and then stabs it abruptly downward into the exercise ball with a loud POP. From there, it's chaos. Hank knocks the computer off

Gary's desk and you start running around the office doing the same to every desk you see. Nothing is safe from the wrath of you and Hank. No family photo, no cup of pens, no jar of decorative stones. The two of you cackle and howl as you completely trash the place. You individually empty every container of leftovers in the fridge onto the break room floor. You knock your standing desk to the ground and watch it fracture with glee. And your ultimate gesture of dominance, you stand on the conference table and spray urine with a ferocity you previously didn't think you were capable of. You look beside you to Hank for approval only to see him doing the same. He's peeing everywhere. Peeing on various locations to claim them as your own has a deep significance where you came from, but Hank is absolutely nailing it on his first try. The two of you pee on everything you can find until you have nothing left to pee.

As you both walk out of the building, carrying the stench of two different species of urine, you can't help but feel liberated. You and Hank amble onto the street and he turns to you laughing, 'Well pal, I don't think you can go back there Monday. So, I guess welcome to early retirement.' Even though what he says should be scary, you don't find yourself feeling too afraid.

'I GUESS I'LL HAVE TO FIND A NEW JOB.'

'What's a wolf need with a job anyway?'

'I DON'T KNOW. I GUESS I JUST THOUGHT THAT'S WHAT HUMANS DO.'

'Well yeah but not because they want to. Nobody *wants* to go to work.'

This seems like a critical detail you could've been informed about much, much earlier in this process.

'WELL, WHAT SHOULD I WANT TO DO?'

'That's up to you my friend, but me personally? I've got a nice little retirement fund saved up and I figured I'd start by buying a houseboat.'

'WHAT EVEN IS THAT?'

'It's just a house that floats.'

'OH MY GOD THAT SEEMS BAD.'

'Yeah but it's actually cool.'

'WHY?'

'I dunno,' he laughs, 'I guess it's just fun to live somewhere you're not supposed to.'

It's been a big day for you. You left a world that didn't feel like your own and entered another that felt like a different version of the same but tonight you left both behind to create something new that's just for you. No matter how long it lasts, no matter how hard it is to maintain, it's yours even if eventually only in memory. Whatever happens next is completely up to you. Plus, you've never been on a boat before.

———

CONGRATULATIONS! You became disenfranchised by corporate America and turned on your employer in an incredible act of defiance. While your human life is in upheaval, you've reached a point where you're excited about your uncertain future.

THE END.

Unbound is the world's first crowdfunding publisher, established in 2011.

We believe that wonderful things can happen when you clear a path for people who share a passion. That's why we've built a platform that brings together readers and authors to crowdfund books they believe in – and give fresh ideas that don't fit the traditional mould the chance they deserve.

This book is in your hands because readers made it possible. Everyone who pledged their support is listed below. Join them by visiting unbound.com and supporting a book today.

The AbiMansour Family

Adam Accardo

Julia Adamson

Arcadia Addams

David Addicott

David H. Adler

Ian Ager

Anna Ahern

Patrick Aitchison

James Alexander

Kate Alexander

Matthew Alexander

Simon Allcott

Maggie Altergott

Josie Altzman

Rez Alvarez

Niel Amundson

Michael Anaya

AC Anderson

Linelle Ann

John Appel

Meg Archer

Rebecca Archer

Damian Arlidge

Angie Arnold

Donna Asher

Jen Aside

Nesher Asner

Greg Atkinson

Dawn Kingsbury Attean

Janna Avon

D B

Evan Bailey

Kendric Bailey

Sandra Bain

Krista Baird

Maxwell Baldridge

Biggus Ballus

Clare Barker

Michael Barks

John Barnabas

Brooke Barnes

Ken Barnes

Will Barnett

Matthew Barr

Sean Barrett

Daniel Braddon Barsby

Paul Bartholow

Catfish Baruni

Benjamin Barush

Jack Bass

Skylar Bastedo

Suzanne Baunsgard

Christine Bazant

Zach Beattie

Bob Beaupre

Nick Bec

James Beck

Joanna Beck

Mason Beets

Aim Beland

Gregory Bell

Kevin Bellardine

Jacob Beloit

Rachel Bennett

Elizabeth Bentley

V. R. Berliner

Ross Berman

Alec Bertram

Laura Bete

Jesse Betend

Jacob Bianchi

Christine Bible

Chris Billett

Glen Birch

Rachel Birrell

Lee Biskin

Kelli Black

Dustin Blackwell

Shaun Blankenship

Nicole Blevins

Matt Blocher

Jacob Block

Bambi Blue

Lauren Blue

Felicia Bock

Adam Boltik

Barbara Bond

Ian Bone

Marcy Bones

Dayna Bongiorno

Kristin Bott

Shaniqua Bowdre

Mx K Bowler

Matthew Brachman

Heather Bradford

Aaron Brady

Dan Brakeley

Tanya Branagan

Kyle Breen

Mike Briggs

Leila ⚡ ⚡ Chillson Brillson

Alice Broadribb

Sarah Brody

Corrianne Brons

Andrew Brooks

Brian Brown

Garrett Brown

Vix Brown

Wesley Brown

Karlin Bruegel

James Bruhns

Gareth Buchaillard-Davies

Marci Burden

Megan Burke

Tom Burns

Michael Burt

Morgan Burton

Jacqui Busch

Kelly Buser

Christie Bush

Liana Buszka

Marcus Butcher

Maeghan Butler

Darryl Byrne

Jeni Bythesea

Jessica Cahill

Lindsay Cahn

Mary & John Cain

Stephanie Cain

Dana Calandrino

Steven Calvert

Ben Campbell

Freddie Campion

Clint Cannon

Sara Cannon

Katie Cantwell

Elion Caplan

Terrill Caplan

David Carch

Jesse Card

Luis Cardenas

Cristy Cardinal

Megan and Rod Carlson

Taylor Carnahan

Dustin Carpenter

Francisco Carretero

Miranda Carson

Adam Carter-Groves

Dawn Cartwright

Kimberly Carvalho

Louis Cashin

Dillon Cassidy

Emily Castillo

Brittany Castonguay

Kevin Castor

Dr. Cat

JC Cat

Michele Catalano

Jim Causey

Adam Cerami

Dean Chambers

Terry Chapman

Heather Chappelle

Spottacus Cheetah

Allen Chen

Lauren Chesnut

Jill Chinchar

Noel Chiotti

Triften Chmil

Elizabeth Christopher

McKinley Churchwell

Diana Claire

Rob Clark

Sarah Clark

Vicky Clenny

Derek Cluck

David Cober

Christopher Coffman

Julie Cohen

Jennie Cole

Cam Collins

Mike Collins

Matthew Conley

John Connelly

James Conner

Thomas Conner

Kathleen Conti

Felix Cook

Thomas Cooke

Renée Corine

David Cornette

Gabriel Cornyn

Megan Corrarino

Cecy Correa

Joey Cosco

Lorna Coupland

Trevin Cox

Scott Craig

Max Roberto Crane

Anthony "illvibe" Craparotta

Ashley Crawford

Rhiannon Creffield

Edel Cribbin

Deborah Crook

Jonathan Crouch

Shawn Crowley

Jon Cunnane

Max Cure-Freeman

Kitty Curran

Craig Curtis

Grace Daly

Damon Damore

Matthew Davidson

Donna Davis

Joshua Davis

James Dawes

Jennifer Dawson

Katz Dawson

Heru de Achaval

Sarah Deady

Alison Deane

Meghan Death

Megan DeCamilla

Donald Deeley

Rebekah Dekker

Alessandro "Doc" Deni

Stuart Denyer

Brennan Depew

Nat Deroin

Sebastien Dessauvage

Stevi Deter

Brian Devey

Darren Devlin

Christian Diaz

Nathaniel Diaz

Thomas Dilligan

Megan Dinosaur

Connor Dixon

Kenny Dolson

Alexandra Donahue

Marcy Donelson

Kate Donnelly

Kayce Dowdy

Bo Dozer

Kat Dragon

Arthur "Torakhan" Dreese

Wendy Drinkwater

Luke Drotar

Kay Dudley

William Dudley

Jacob Duffner

dwwolf

Corey Dyke

Melissa Ebbe

Dash Eberhart

Joseph Edwards

Stephanie Edwards

John Eide

Anna Maria Eilertsen

Jason Eliaser

Jamie Elliott

Ike Ellsworth

Eloquar

Louis Emmett

Maria English

Collin Estell

Chris Etches

Anna Evans

Shelly Evans

Lisa Fagundes

Amy Fairbrother

David Falkner

Derek Fan

Fanboat

Erika Fant

Karen Farrington

David Fayram

Anne Feher

Teasha Feldman-Fitzthum

Laura A. Fenton

Morgan Ferdinand

Mark Ferreira

Carolyn Fiddler

Alenka Figa

Aleta Figurelli

Kiaza Fillmore

Matthew Finch

Rebecca Fiore

Jessica Fisher

Melissa Fix

Tanya Fleming

Jessica Fletcher

Ellen Flint

David Foradori

Joanna Forbes

Owen Ford

Doug Fort

Anna Fowler

Ashley Fox

Diana Fox

Nick Frampton

Daniël Franke

Amy Franz

Marco Frazee

Jason Freeman

Sarah Freeman

Sara Freid

John Freriks

Adrienne Friend

Desirae Friesen

Rebecca Friesen

Naomi Fritts

Victor Frost

Devin James Fry

Ali Fyffe

Julie Gagnon

Sky Gaidosik

Davin Galbraith

Ramuel Gall

Annemarie Gallagher

Lawrence Gallagher

Maggie Gallagher

Antero Garcia

Ana Garcia Jimenez

Morgan Gard

Leslie Gardner

Desiree Garrett

Melissa Gay

Dylan Geile

Warden S. Gentles

Kelsey George

Fuzzy Gerdes

Dimitry Gershenson

Johannie Gervais

David Gian-Cursio

Arden Giangarra

Marina Gibbons

Pete Gill

Joanna Gillespie

Stuart Gillespie

Jessica Ginting

Melissa Glasscock

Julia Glassman

Miriam Glassman

Amanda Gleason

Cooper Glodoski

Kristen Glomv

Tara Glover

James Gold

Raquel Goldman

Scott Goldstein

Jennifer Goloboy

Samael Goode

Stephanie Goodner

James Goodwin

Andrea Gordon

Erin Gordon

Anamika Goree

Moragh Goyette

Adrianne Grady

Rachel Green

Gavin "Possibly a Wolf"
  Greene

John Gregorcic

Christopher Griego

Mike Griffiths

Richard Gropp

Gabriel Grossman

Catherine Grubb

Kyle Gunby

Angela Gunn

Brianne Gutmann

Luke Gutzwiller

Kateland Haas LaVigne

Joshua Hackett

Joseph Hadley

Aarica Hamilton

Cynthia Hanby

Kaylie Hanna

Sarena Hansel

Bob Harbin

Ian Hardacre & Lily Nichol

James Harnois

Lucas Harrington

Carl Harris

Kamila Harris

Mark Harrison

Michele Hartsuiker

David Harvey

Kaitlin Hassett

Andrea Haverdink

Stuart Hawkes

Martin Hawkins

Julia Hayes

Angie Hayes-Yousif

Pure Heart

Kyle Heaton

Martin Hecko

Jeremy Hedlund

Mikey Heller

Jeremy Hellwig

Kate Henderson

Charlotte Henkle

Kate Henriques

Solange Henson

Garion Herman

Mauricio Hernandez

Barbara Herodes

Michael Heron

Angelina Hewitt

Sophia Hewitt

Gwyneth Hibbett

Kaitlyn Higa

Max Higgins

Chris Hill

Fiona Hill

Casey Hills

Bob Hoag

Austin Hofeman

Tory Hoffman

James Hogan

Kali Holder

Jonathon Holland

E S Holmans

Geo Holms

Cynthia Hong

Brandon Hood

Chris Hopson

David Hormell

Meredith Horning-Rao

Pat Howard

Daisie Huang

April Hudson

Shawn Hudson

Adrian Hughes

Claire Hugman

Miroslav Hundak

Andrew Hungerford

Jennie Huntoon

Shayne Husbands

Tom Hutchings

Jennifer Ibrahim

Mariya Ignatyeva

Q Illespont

Alexis Iwanisziw

Bonnie Jackson

Tyler Jackson

Jean Jacobsen

Sara Jaffer

Kyle Janis

Madeline Jarboe

Franny Jay

Kate Jeffery

Amy L. Jenkins

Jay Jernigan

JGD

Shea Johns

Brian Johnson

Hunter Johnson

Lauren Johnson

Trent Johnson

Emmy Maddy Johnston

Amanda Jones

Kris Jones

Jeff Jonker

H.C. Joseph

Stacie Joy

Phoebe Juel

Stephanie Juergens

Juniper Nest

E & V JW

Meredith Kachel

Max Kaehn

Liam Kane

Nikolas Katrick

Kaitlyn Kauffman

Chris Kaye

Michael Keefner

Morgan Keeler

Jen Kehoe

Andy Keith

Katharine Kelly

Rachel Kelly

Samuel Kelly

Kelsey

Adam Kennedy

Conrad Kenney

Kevin Kenny

Alexander Kerckhoff

Daniel Key

Dan Kieran

Matt Kilens

Fiona Kilfoyle

Robert King

The King's School Library
(Canterbury)

Chris Kingsley

Robert Kinns

Brian Kirkland

Emily Kirkpatrick

Matthew Kitzi

Rachael Klapko

Kat Kline

Trevor Knoblich

Alexander Koch

Sky Komenda

Matthew Kremske

Brian Krulik

Seth Kalela Kugler

Melissa Louise Kuhn

Anna Kuipers

Jessica Kulak

Amy Kulow-Taylor

Sam Kumar

Russ L

Jalynn L.

Erika Lachapelle

Mary Lafferty

Anna LaForge

Mit Lahiri

Noel Lairson

Madeline Laizure

Eon Lajoie

Holly Lakey

Ionuț Lala

Aaron Lamour

Alicia Lampkin

Veronica Landa

Cherry Lane

Nathan Langenkamp

Sarah Lapré

Ann Larimer

Julia Larsen

Kate Larson

Elizabeth Last

Emily Lauer

Nate Law

Lawn

Jack Lawrence

Richard Lawson

Lori Leaumont

Marc Lebailly

Jacqueline Lee

Tyler Lee

Bill Leetch

Annie Lepage

Jessica Lerner

Annabel Lewis

Karen Lewis

Alex Lien

Georgia Lillie

Sandra Lindquist

Jeanine Lindsay

Amanda Ling

Jonathan Lloyd

Diane Loborec

Christine Locher

Gratchen Locke

Rob Loftis

Ashley Lopez

Elise Lorene

Katie Louis

Oddvar Lovaas

Lindsay Love

Travis Love

Phillip Lu

Nathan Lutchansky

Steve Lutz

Chris Lyden

Adam Lyzniak

Elise Mac Adam

Pete MacAskill

Madeline MacDonald

Simon MacDonald

Elizabeth Mackey

Dawn Magyar

Sheila Majumdar

Jade Mallon

Drew Malone

Sarah Manuel

Christianne Manzano

Braed Mape-Brown

Robert Marchand

Meghan Marie

Mirri Markwitz

Owen Marshall

Esther Martijn

Katie Martin

SR Martin

Mario Martinez

Justin Mashburn

Charlie Mason

RS Mason

Laura Mast

Vivien Mast

Lori Matsumoto

Ben Matthews

Indigo Maughn

Kate Mauldin

Anthony May

Sam May

Jessica Maybury

Patrick Mc Rae

Zenia McAllister

Katherine McCormack

Rae McEdward

Elliott McEldowney

Morgan McFarland

Ryan McGee

Milo McGehee

Kevin McGinn

Michael McGuire

Brittany McIntyre

Heidi McIver

Brittany McLaughlin

Kate McNulty

Heather McTiernan

Brennan Mcveigh

Joel Meador

Brian Mendonca

Calvin Metcalf

Elly Meyers

David Middleton

Andrew Mihalevich

Anne Millar

Christopher Miller

Millie

Matt Mills

Sarah Mills

Jonathan Millsap

John Mitchinson

Josh Modell

Dom Mofford

Sandra Molteni

Darragh Mondoux

Daniel Monroe

Scott Montague

Beth Montague-Hellen

Katherine Montalto

Karina Montgomery

Miranda Montooth

Diego Montoyer

Helix Moore

James Moore

Nick Moore

Tyler Moore

James Morgan

Jamie Morgan

Daria Morgendorffive

Jehanne Morreaux

Michael Morris

Eli Morris-Heft

Matthew W Morse

Kelsey Morse-Brown

Gregory Moses

Javier Muhrer

Emily Muir

Ari Multhauf

Mike Mulvey

Rich Mulvey

Robin Mulvihill

Katrina Murphy

Alex Murr

Ricky Musci

Jay Myers

Al Napp

Timo Nappa

Carlo Navato

Marilyn Necci

Suzy Needle

Ali Neer

Wendy Nehring

Stuart Neilson

Tom Nelson

Matt Neubauer

Daniel Newland

Ömer Ney

Vero Ng

Chris Nguyen

Tyler Nickerson

Abigail Nicole

Jeff Niemczura

Ellen Noble

Nathan Nolan

Jake Noll

Jenna Nunziato

Melynda Nuss

Kyrie O'Connor

Chris O'Donnell

Kate O'Shea

David O'Sullivan

Kara O'Donovan

Kerrie Obermeyer

Theodor Olaussen

Chris Olean

Andrew Oleniach

Rosalie Oliver

Joshua Olsen

Katie Olson

Lara Olstad

Nicholas Omland

Joe Ondrechen

Lynn Oneacre

Ingrid Oomen

Alyssa Opiela

Corn Michael Osborne

Laura Osterbrock

Farallon Otter

Frank Otto

Nate Otto

Richie Owens

Christopher Palmer

Kenneth Palmgren

Lucas Papadopoulos

Jeanne Park

Amara G. Parker

Hilary Parker

Drew Parroccini

Susan Parrott

Julie Pascal

Jonathan Pasley

Nicholas Pasquale

Mitch Patterson

Molly Benjamin Patterson

Varghese Paul

Genna Paulsen

Allison Pauly

Leah Peasley

Jon Peck

Jennifer Peers

Cynthia Pelston

Manda Pepper Langlinais

Jonathan Perrine

Bruce Perry

Ryan Perry

Zach Peterson

Christopher Petrilli

Charity A. Petrov

Mark Phaedrus

Ingrid Philigret

Sarah Phim

Piotr "ThePiachu" Piasecki

Marko Pichlak

Alexander J Pierce

Oleg Piltsin

Jacob Pinholster

Jonathan Pirro

Nicola Pocock

Justin Pollard

Jonathan Pomeroy

Christopher Pope

Wendy Posson

James Post

Kaela Rose Power

Arielle Powers

Shaun Presow

Alicia Pretot

Paige Pritchard

Nadia Proctor

Chris Pugh

Marley Pullinger

Aimee Quenneville

Kevin Quick

Brand Rackley

Liza Radley

Angela Raisedbywolves

Anna Rankin

Gevyn Rasco

Deb Blakley Rasmussen

Anthony Ravago III

Kelsey Raymond

Kevin Reed

Lauren Reed

Garth D. Reese

Leanne Reich

Katherine Repage

Mike Reyes

Aaron Reynolds

Valerie Rice

Janelle Rich

Patricia Riggs

Bryce Riley

Colleen Riley

Ian Riley

Liam Riley

Phaedra Riley

Stephanie Rinehart

Jennifer Rinella Moskal

Axel Ringwood

Jason Risk

Ewen Roberts

Kate Roberts

Shadrock Roberts

Kevin Robinson

Amy Robson

Montgomery Robson

Doug Rockney

Dominic Rodriguez

Donna Rodriguez

Lisa Rodriguez

Blaine Roever

Ethan Rogers

Jarvellis Rogers

Sarah Rohr

Erin Rollman

Rondo

Stuart Room

Stan and Robbie RosenThom

Rebecca Ross

Laura Roth

Kaitlin Rounds

Dan Rounzie

Dr. Betsy E.E. Rowe

Georgie Rowe

Nathan Rowe

Cara Roxanne

Katie Royer

Guillermo Ruiz Henares

Joe Ruscio

Bonnie Russell

Robert S

Michael Salvia

Daniela Sanchez

Susan Sandenaw

Anthony Sanders

Ben Sandler

Cary Sandvig

Robbie Sassetti

Valerie Sather

Tom Savage

Lisa Scanlon

Deborah Schauffler

Kaley Schenk

Bastien Scher

L Scherer

Jenni Schimmels

Galen Schmidt

Noah Schnaubelt

Jacob Schonberg

Terri Schultz

Rachel Schwalbach

Maximillian Schwanekamp

Jon Schwarzbauer

Bruce Scott

David Scott

Jean Scully

Myra Sefton

Paul Segovich

Ryan Sellers

Andrew Sempere

Jamon Serrano

Dave Severenuk

Vikram Shah

Shanna

Sarah Sharp

Becca Sheehan

Diane & Jim Sheehan

Linda Sheehan

Mary Sheehan Steinmetz

James Sheppard

Emma Shirey

Jordan Shiveley

Kristi Shmyr

Ethan Shroll

Thomas Siddons

Nick Sidlin

Lauren Siegert

Marshall Sigsby

Adam Simon

Scott Sinclair

K.A. Sinervo

Flannery Skadberg

McLeod Skinner

Adam Skroh

Tif Slama

Peter Smallridge

Damon Smith

Devin Smith

Lindsay Smith

Melinda Smith

Susan Smith Webb

Tyler Snodgrass

Anna Snyder

Kathleen Snyder

Marie Sobieski

Jeff Soules

Scott Sousa & Kristina Jameson

Júlia Souza

Katie Sowder

Jay Sparke

Michelle Spies

Connor Stack

Maddie Stansell

Jack Stapleton

Jeremy Stark

Will Starms

Niklas Starow

Lydia Starring

Jill Stauffer

Erica Steele

Jessica Steele-Sanders

Dyon Stefanon

Joe Steiert

Kurt & Abby Stein

Susie Steinbach

Matthew Stephens

David Stevens

Sandy Stith

Ryan Stivers

Daniel Stock

Jeremy Stoll

Tyson Stolte

Claire Stone

Laura E Storey

Cecelia Story

Greg Stovall

Jeremiah Strack

David Stroud

Laura Stump

Morgan Sturgill

Louis Stutz

Anne Sullivan

Erin Summers

Valerie Summey

Zane Suttmore

Christopher Swenson

Andrew Swinehart

Drew Talley

Tangles

Brandy Tannahill

Jim Taylor

Madison Taylor-Hayden

TBTay

Jillian Tees

Joshua Tehee

Max Temkin

Scott Templeton

Amy Tennery

Maja Thalling

Adrien Thebo

Jerry Thell

Ross Theriault

Tasha Thomas

Brandy Thompson

Alexa Thorne

Tanya Thornton

Autumn Tibbits

Ray Ting

Beverly Tjerngren

Casimir Tokarski

Mary Tooley

Russ Tooley

Bo Törnros

Marion Tout

Ross Tregaskis

Joshua Trein

Andrew Trembley

G. Michael Truran

Maria Trusmei

Patrick Tunney

Benjamin Turner

Trey Turner

Tim Unrath

Clive Upton

Christopher Urquhart

Nichole Valdez

Nikka Valken

John Van Ginkel

Brian Van Meter

Mary Van Tyne

Johan van Voskuilen

John VanDeBrook

Brian Vander Veen

Geoffrey Vankirk

Eldon Vaselaar

Charlie Vergos

Trueth Verou

Joshua Villagomez

Yury Voronin

Leo Vrana

Jon W, Chicago

Evelyn Wake

Damon L. Wakes

Matthew Walker

Dustin Wallace

Jake Wallach

Eleanor Walsh

Elisa Walsh

Kieran Walsh

Liz Walsh

Ellie Warmington

Megan Warner

Shane Waskiewich

Whitney Wasson

Dan Weatherford

Vicki Weathersby

Jordan Webb

K Webb

Benjamin Weber

Gregory Weber

Rachel Weeks

Matthew Weichert

Chris Weigert

Adam Weintraub

Megan Weireter

Cassidy Werner

Sarah Rhea Werner

Trent Westbrook

Roo Wetzel

James White

Walter H. White

Brock Wilbur

Jacob Wilfong

Haley Williams

Catherine Williamson

James Willsey

Steven Wilson

Peregrin Winkle

Corbett Winningham

Clark Winters

Tom Wisdom

Katarzyna Wiszniewska

Maya Witters

Jacob Wolf

Kit Wolf

Marcus A Wolf

Mike Wolf

Nesheph Wolf

Valerie Wolf

WolffyTheReal

Johnny Wolfsberger

Johann Wolovich

Evan Wood

Matthew Wood

Zac Wood

Melinda Woodard

Meg Woodrum

Alexandros Worgan

David Wright

Christine Wu

Heather Wylie

Stephen Wylie

XaosWolf

Hanna Yang

Joseph A. Yencich

Jessica Yonker

W. York

Fred Yost

Aubrey Young

James Young

Ian Yule

Stephanie Zabinski

Daniel Zambrano.

Adel Zeller

Julie Zeraschi

Vulpes Zerda

Michele Zorrilla

Emily Zuckerman

Nick Zupancic